CRAZY ABOUT KURT

A Novel

By

Will Link

To Praveen, Larissa, Pete, J.T., Sean and all the rest of my Long Island friends past and present. This book is for all of you.

T.J.

All T.J. Weber cared about was if he had time for another cigarette. He didn't even have his usual nicotine obsessive urge for another one, but it would be something to do. Something better than walking up the hill, back towards the school to take yet another chemistry test he knew he'd fail. A month ago, when his guidance counselor informed him that he would be back next year for 13th grade, T.J. made the logical decision to totally check out. It seemed completely counterproductive for her to tell him this. What motivation did he have to even try anymore? Was his future written in stone? Was it all so hopeless?

And yet T.J. still thought he should go through the motions. He'd show up to receive his F. He flicked the butt into the street and headed back onto school property.

Smithtown High School used to have a smoking section called "The Pit," where students during lunch hours or between classes could squeeze in a smoke. But along the way an administrator, or more likely a meddling parent, decided that having a smoking section encouraged addictive behavior. Now teenagers were forced to trek a quarter mile through the parking lot to stand just on the other side of school property. If you had even one foot on the property a security guard, who usually had a cigarette dangling from their lips as well, would force you to take a step back. What was the fucking point? The same students were still going off to smoke but now they were all just late for class. If anything, even more students were now smoking. The long walk was a great way to avoid responsibility. Sure, it sucked in the winter, trudging through snow and the cold air to get a few drags in, but it didn't stop anyone. It was now April. There was still a chill, but on this early afternoon the sun was shining. It must have been the warmest day so far this year.

T.J. marched past the other so called "dirtbags." He knew that's what most of his classmates considered him as well. However, it was much more complicated than that. His persona contained unique traits from a variety of cliques. He had greasy long hair and liked to smoke weed but he wasn't a "stoner kid." He didn't even own a skateboard, and every stoner kid owns a skateboard. The stoners would be the first to agree that T.J. was too angry to be one of them. He had the anger of a "punk kid." But his musical taste was not punk, as evidenced by the KMFDM *Angst* t-shirt he was wearing. After all, more than any other clique weren't punk kids defined by their musical taste? Hell, their entire subculture was named after a style of music. Did his love of German industrial metal make him more Goth? But he wasn't really Goth either, was he? Despite the black t-shirt, black jeans and black Doc Marten boots, he very rarely wore his spiked dog collar or lipstick. It was all very confusing and probably led to some sort of pathetic high school identity crisis. Being a teenager was hard.

Finally, T.J. reached the school's front entrance. Even without having that second cigarette he was going to be late. What a fucking waste. If he was going to walk into a test late he should have at least rewarded himself with more smokes. Suddenly, a high-pitched shriek pierced the silence. Stopping dead in his tracks he turned towards the noise, just as the shriek became a full-on hysterical wail. It was coming from a girl in a nice, yellow spring dress. Her hair was pulled back in a ponytail, tears pouring down her cheeks, ruining her makeup. T.J. struggled to think of her name. Sandy? Betty? He knew it ended in a "y" and that she had been in a health class with him two years ago. She ran in different circles and until this embarrassing scene, he had never found her interesting enough to remember her name.

Betty/Sandy shook violently while being held by a girl wearing a flannel and jeans. This second girl looked like someone T.J. should know, but didn't. She looked like a dirtbag. Shit, now he was the one boxing people into cliques unfairly. The girl in flannel tried to calm this hysterical student, but the tears kept coming, her face turning bright red. T.J. figured the right thing to do would be to make sure everyone was o.k. Plus, at this point, he was just too curious not to know what happened.

"Is everything alright?"

"Kurt Cobain is dead," the flannel-wearing girl blurted out, almost offended by the question.

"What?"

"He killed himself."

These words caused Betty/Sandy to scream in horror, a reminder that her generation had just lost the closest thing they had to a voice.

T.J. took the news in. He knew what Kurt Cobain and Nirvana meant to everyone at the school. He knew the rest of the day, as this information spread, students would be in a state of depression worse than any song the pioneering grunge band had ever released. He knew no work would get done, that Betty/Sandy wasn't the only one who would be overcome with emotion. He knew that the world would never be the same.

But most of all, he knew he had found a way out of his chemistry test!

This was the best excuse to get an early start on the weekend. Because T.J. couldn't give two shits about Kurt Cobain. He found his music whiny. To him bands like Nine Inch Nails made misanthropy angrier and sexier. Other than the time he masturbated to the anarchy cheerleaders from the "Smells Like Teen Spirit" music video, Nirvana had offered him little release from his teenage angst. Until now.

"Fuck it," T.J. declared.

He turned around and headed back towards the property line, popping a cigarette in his mouth and lighting it in front a security guard. Who was going to stop him? Kurt Cobain had just died.

Jackie

She couldn't believe the news. He was dead. She would never get to see him perform. Never get to hear him play her favorite song of his, "In Bloom," live. Her friend Jeff was the only person she knew who had actually seen Nirvana in concert, nearly a year earlier at Roseland. Regret and envy began to consume her. She was supposed to go to that show but her mom was being a real bitch about letting her take the train into the city alone. At the time it wasn't worth the fight. Now she'd give anything to fight that fight.

Jackie Spampinato was in a state of shock over Kurt Cobain's death. Life was so precious and here she was, wasting it in a calculus class. A class she didn't even need in order to graduate. That said, she was keeping it together a lot better than some of her fellow classmates.

Whenever Jackie would get drunk at a party, which she rarely did, she'd usually lean into her drunkenness. Embracing the booze made her feel like she didn't have a worry in the world. Inevitably, however, she'd run into someone who was sloppy drunk. An annoying mess of a human being who'd be spilling their drink and vomiting on the carpet. This would only make her realize just how drunk she *wasn't* and immediately sober her up. It turned out grief worked the same way. As upset as Jackie was, it was impossible to lean into sadness with Mandy Simmons around.

Mandy could not stop crying. From the second class started she was either sniffling loudly or breaking out into a full-blown sob. In her pretty yellow dress Mandy didn't look like a typical Nirvana fan. Jackie wasn't going to make that sort of judgment though. Some would say that other than the single Manic Panic streak of blue in her own brunette hair, you might not think of her as a grunge fan. Maybe Mandy had a family member who'd also killed themselves and this brought back those memories. Or maybe she just loved Kurt Cobain.

Mr. Arden was less understanding. He was always one of the more serious educators. If you were a second late to class, even if you had a pass from another teacher, he'd give you a hard time. Math seemed to be the only thing he cared about. What a sad life. They were ten minutes into class and Mr. Arden's frustration was boiling over. Did he honestly expect them to concentrate on math problems when a man they all admired was dead?

Stepping away from a problem on the chalkboard, Mr. Arden turned towards Mandy.

"I'm going to need you to save...*all this*, for after class."

Clearly embarrassed to be put on the spot, Mandy broke out into an even louder sob. Mr. Arden stood his emotionless ground.

"You didn't even know him. This is an AP class and we have a lot of work before the Regents."

Jackie was disgusted. She looked around at her classmates. Stone-faced. Either too caught up in their own emotions or too afraid to stand up for themselves. Would no one say anything? Mandy was now crying uncontrollably. Rather than pity, Mr. Arden looked down at her with the same level of disdain Jackie had towards him.

"She's sad. Let her be sad," Jackie finally blurted out. Mr. Arden seemed shocked. Here was one of his better students questioning his authority.

"Excuse me?"

"I get that calculus is important, but so is Nirvana. None of us are going to be able to concentrate today, so just let us be sad."

"Miss Spampinato, I appreciate that you're trying to look out for your fellow classmate, but I have a job to do. Teach. And you have a job to do. Learn. And those jobs are more important than a dead drug addict."

"No! They're not!" she continued to protest.

"Tell me then, why was Mr. Cobain so important?"

Jackie had never argued like this with an authority figure. Again, it usually wasn't worth the fight. This was uncharted territory. And now she was backed into a corner. Flustered. Why was Kurt Cobain so important? How do you answer a question like that? Art is emotional. When you look at a painting by Monet or Picasso, how the hell are you supposed to put into words the way it makes you feel? Why should you even have to? And lyrics about pretty songs and singing along and shooting guns worked the same way, even if you don't know what it means.

"He...he just *was!*"

That's all the argument Jackie could muster. However, she knew she had to make a bigger statement than that. The whole class was looking at her. Looking to her. Even Mandy had finally stopped crying. Jackie was now the one carrying the class's collective pain.

She stood up, made a big show of collecting her books, and stormed out of the classroom.

"Miss Spampinato! Miss Spampinato! Get back here!"

*****

Jackie had never cut a class before, but this whole day had put her in a funk. Mr. Arden was right. None of them knew Kurt Cobain, did they even have a right to be upset? Most of ninth period Jackie spent in the common area. Sure, she could have left early and gone to Seth's house as was tradition. Cutting class was one thing, but leaving the school grounds was something else entirely. Jackie liked the idea that she smoked and drank and fucked but at the same time held a 3.8 GPA and was going to NYU in the fall. She could "have it all."

What she wanted most of all right now was a Coke. The vending machine had other ideas. It wouldn't accept her crinkled-up dollar bill. She had repeatedly tried straightening it along the side of the machine, but every time she'd insert it, it'd shoot back out. Frustrated, Jackie began pushing the vending machine, then banging her small fists against it.

"Be careful," a voice from behind her said. "Two hundred and fifty people a year are killed by vending machines falling on them."

Jackie knew the voice well. It was Jeff Rosenduft.

"I find that statistic hard to believe," she said.

"It's true. That's why all vending machines have warning stickers on them." Jeff pointed to a sticker plastered on the machine's side. A stick figure being crushed by a vending machine. He then pulled a dollar out of his wallet and inserted it. With a smile, Jackie got her Coke. She tried to hand Jeff her wrinkled-up buck, but Jeff waved her off. She didn't fight him on it.

"So," she started. "Kurt."

"I don't think I've processed it yet," Jeff said. "There was a lot going on even before this. And the teachers are trying to talk about it, which feels so fake. It's not their loss, it's our loss."

"It *is* our loss," Jackie said, just coming to this realization. Who cares if she didn't know Kurt, she loved the music. "The teachers are talking about it? Because Arden was being a real dick to us."

"Wow," Jeff said, surprised. "Most of the adults I've seen today are walking on eggshells, afraid we're all going to start killing ourselves."

Jeff was the very person Jackie needed to see right now. He understood.

"Hey," he continued. "The Freaks are opening for The Scofflaws tonight. Are you going?"

"I was planning on—"

BEEP BEEP BEEP

Jackie was interrupted by her beeper. This was happening more and more frequently, and her friends were starting to find the device a real nuisance. Maybe not as much a nuisance as the person beeping her. Jeff glanced down at the page:

143

"So it's love?" he asked.

Was it love? Jackie wasn't sure what it was, but she'd been dating Sean Greco since New Year's Eve when they met at a party. He was a sophomore at Stony Brook University, the closest college to Smithtown. Her friend Maureen had a sister who went there, so they were able to crash a New Year's party in the dorms. Sean stood out from the manic high school boys she'd usually party with. He had a laidback attitude with his backwards Phish hat, sitting in the corner twirling a lacrosse stick in his hands. He was also disgustingly handsome. Blonde, tan and far more muscular then the wimpy high school string beans she usually dated. Sometime after midnight Jackie played him in beer pong. She was pretty sure he let her win, but the gesture was nice. Maybe the only nice thing he'd done for her in the three months they'd been dating. Sure, he was paging her "I love you" but how genuine is a page anyway? Can love be expressed in a series of numbers?

"I wouldn't call it love, but things are...*good*," Jackie said.

"You're clearly lying," Jeff replied.

"I just don't like you or anyone judging me or my relationships."

"Fine. Do you need to call him back or do you want to head over to Seth's with me?"

Jeff didn't have a beeper. If he did he'd know you only needed to call someone back if they beeped you 911 to denote an emergency or 424 which meant "call me back." Beepers had their own language, and Jackie had quickly mastered it. 143 was "I love you." The numbers stood for the amount of letters in each word. You could tell someone you were thinking of them with a simple 823. Jackie preferred this because it was still sweet but far less serious. Any elementary school student using a calculator could figure out 07734 was "hello" and 1*177155*400 was "I miss you." In one way it was great to be so connected to everyone. Someone could contact Jackie at literally any time. If there was an actual emergency, she would know about it immediately. In another way this technology was a real pain in the ass. Sean didn't have a normal schedule. Some days he'd have three classes, some days one. So when he was in his dorm room drinking beers and smoking pot, he'd start paging Jackie. And she didn't always have the time to make it to a payphone to call or beep him back. What was the etiquette? If she didn't respond was she being a bitch? When Jackie was little her father had a phone installed in his car. It seemed like the stupidest idea. Why did he think he was so important that he needed to be reached at all times? Jackie's father was no one important. He was just some fucking guy who worked at a bank and easily bought into new gimmicks. However, one night when he got a flat tire on the Long Island Expressway, he was able to call a tow truck. That was certainly something to think about every time Jackie started to complain about her beeper. Though some alone time would be nice. Maybe next week she'd leave her beeper at home. What was Sean going to do? Dump her? He didn't care enough to do that, and neither did she. Despite the 143, she knew they were just passing the time.

The bell signaling the end of the school day finally rang. In seconds the halls would be filled with students racing towards their cars or buses.

"Nah," Jackie said. "Let's just go to Seth's."

Matt

Billy Joel.

If Matt Pace were being honest, his favorite musician was Billy Joel.

Why should he feel shame about this? First of all Matt lived on Long Island. And who was more synonymous with Long Island than Billy Joel? At any given time of day a Billy Joel song would be playing on the radio. Turn on WALK 97.5 or 102.3 WBAB right now and Matt would bet money you'd hear Billy Joel. Billy had such a deep, personal Long Island history too. Matt's father went to Hicksville High School with him, although they ran in different circles. T.J. Weber claimed that his absentee father, John, was in fact the John at the bar in the song "Piano Man." Matt had been to see Billy play at Nassau Colosseum four times, and when he was young his mother used to play 8-tracks of his music constantly. But the real reason he was Matt's favorite musician was the storytelling.

Billy Joel painted such vivid stories in his songs, with characters Matt understood. Blue collar workers, religious young girls, drunks who missed out on their dreams. His favorite was "Scenes From an Italian Restaurant." The epic seven-minute-and-thirty-seven-second song is divided into three unique parts, one of which tells the story from the high to the low for a couple of high school sweethearts named Brenda and Eddie. Matt saw Brenda and Eddie in almost every middle-aged couple he knew, including some couples close to home.

Matt wanted to be a filmmaker and he understood storytelling was the most important part of that process. Why bother to make a film if you don't have a great story to tell? Listening to those 8-

tracks in his mom's car was Matt's earliest exposure to storytelling, and it always stayed with him.

But he couldn't go around telling his peers Billy Joel was his favorite musician.

Sure, ten years ago no one would have batted an eye. Every kid in elementary school just liked whatever their parents exposed them to. Here in high school everyone developed their own musical tastes. They moved on to listen to Pearl Jam, Alice in Chains and Nirvana. Matt stuck by Billy. It's not that he disliked Nirvana, but Matt wasn't into subtlety. He didn't know what half of Nirvana's lyrics meant. They were telling a story, but it was with muddled metaphors of alienation. So as much as Matt might enjoy rocking out to the music they made, he could never gain a clear understanding of it. Don't disguise what you're saying, just come right out and fucking say it. That way everyone will understand. Billy Joel did that.

Today was going to be a hard day for Nirvana fans and an even harder day for people who pretended to be bigger fans than they were. Matt owned none of Nirvana's albums, but before the day was over he'd be sure to make a tape of *Nevermind*. He wanted to be part of the conversation. It's all anyone was talking about. Including right now in class.

Miss Chlystun, his English teacher, was in her early thirties. Although Matt understood in the grand scheme of things this wasn't that old, it still felt ancient to him. Being one of the younger teachers at school unfortunately didn't make her attractive. Miss Chlystun was sweet but homely. Matt had heard myths about schools where there were actual hot teachers. What a welcome distraction that would be. To spend the forty-five minutes of class time fantasizing about what was going on under a teacher's dress rather than actually having to listen to them. As hard as he tried,

Matt had never been attracted to any of his educators. Smithtown High School had no hot teachers.

Matt was looking up at the chalkboard where Miss Chlystun had written four words.

mulatto, albino, mosquito, libido

"Now what do you think these words meant to Kurt in the context of the song? Anyone?" Miss Chlystun asked.

She had decided to throw out today's lesson plan and talk only about Kurt Cobain. In one way it was cool of her to try and break down the lyrics to "Smells Like Teen Spirit" as if it were any other poem or piece of literature they discussed. In another way it felt pandering. Who knows? Matt could have sworn he caught her wiping away a tear. Maybe Nirvana did mean something to her?

The class was not engaged. They just stared up at her blankly. Were they too heartbroken to answer? Or were they simply too embarrassed to answer wrong? Here was a song they had all listened to a million times and purported to love. How could they not know what it meant? This just reinforced Matt's argument. How great could a song be if its intended audience couldn't decipher its meaning? Miss Chlystun was forced to continue on her own.

"Alienation. Think about it. A mulatto. An albino. These are people that feel like outsiders. A mosquito. A reviled blood-sucking creature. My libido. Something primal you can't always control or understand. Kurt felt like an outsider. Felt reviled. Uncontrollable. Teenagers feel like outsiders. Teenagers don't understand themselves."

This analysis made sense. An intelligent point that could be repeated later on when the inevitable discussion of Nirvana came up among friends.

*****

So far senior year had been Matt's favorite. Mostly, because for the first time in his academic life, he was able to do whatever he wanted. He had already earned all the credits in math and science, two subjects he had very little comprehension of, that he needed in order to graduate. He'd decided on going to a state school, so college wasn't an issue. With all that settled, Matt could devote five whole periods a day to working on his video projects.

Mrs. Benson, the film and video teacher, basically let Matt, along with Jeff Rosenduft, have run of the room and all the equipment whenever they wanted. Jeff, who was head editor of the school's video yearbook, even had a key to the room. That way he could come in early and work on projects. He'd often pick up Matt on the way in so he could work as well. In their junior year Jeff and Matt cut a deal with the athletic department. For credit, rather than have to go to gym once a day, get all sweaty and show how terrible at sports they were, the video department would start a program to tape the school's sporting events. That way coaches could review the tapes and figure out how to improve the team. Thus the sports video program was born, and Matt would never again have to get undressed in front of a group of boys.

Matt knew that he was leaving a lasting mark on the school. Everyone knew who he was. He was the video guy. He'd wander the halls, lugging a VHS camcorder around, constantly capturing footage that would be used in the school's video yearbook. When he wasn't doing that he was filming short scripts around the building. Little stories about student life he'd come up with. Matt had recently penned a comedy, a cautionary tale about two fat kids who bullied one another. It was actually based on two real-life students at the school and he briefly worried they'd find out and kick his ass. Jeff, on the other hand, took a more cinéma vérité approach. He loved to capture real reactions. Like the time he organized a surprise dance party in the cafeteria and slowly got everyone to join in. Or when he filmed their friend Tariq passing out free blow pops. What was so great about that piece was how untrusting his fellow students were of accepting free candy. It really said something honest about human nature. How people have trouble accepting generosity with nothing asked in return. Jeff won an award at the Hudson Valley Student Film Festival for it. Matt attended the ceremony.

Yes, Matt and Jeff ruled the film and video department. Deep down, however, Matt was troubled by the knowledge that Jeff was better than him. It's why Jeff got the keys to the room and Matt just tagged along. It's why Jeff was going to a fancy film school in Manhattan and Matt was going to SUNY New Paltz. Matt didn't hate Jeff for his success. Instead Matt hated himself for his own fears. Jeff was shooting for the stars where Matt was too content being a big fish in a small pond. He'd rather be the best filmmaker on Long Island than ever venture to Hollywood where he'd be just one voice lost in a sea of thousands. He'd read about a film that recently played at the Sundance Film Festival. The whole thing took place entirely within a convenience store and was supposedly hilarious. The director, who was also from the tri-state area, had paid for it by maxing out credit cards. Matt wondered if he could ever be that gutsy. Probably not. So rather than even apply to school with Jeff—or dare he dream, a school out in Los Angeles—Matt was comfortable spending the next four years in upstate New York. He'd continue being a somebody. The king of New Paltz film!

It was halfway through ninth period. Matt was sitting, quietly editing a video of girls playing field hockey. The coach was retiring and as a sports video project, Matt agreed to put together a highlight reel in her honor. There were worse things he could be doing than watch athletic girls in skirts run around a field. He'd slowly toggle through the footage, carefully finding his in point and marking it. Then he'd even more slowly toggle to his out point. Matt would be willing to murder everyone in the school and burn the building to the ground, just for a chance to see what was under those skirts.

The door to the video room opened and in walked Tariq Sherani. Matt considered Tariq kind of a sidekick. A smart but quiet friend who was pretty much always available to help out in any way. You needed a lift? Tariq would drive. You wanted to go to the movie? Tariq would join you. You needed someone to pick up condoms for you at the store? Tariq would do that too. Matt swiveled around in his chair, smile across his face, happy to see him. Wait a minute. Suddenly the smile turned to a frown. What the hell was Tariq wearing?

Tariq had on a t-shirt with a flying saucer, accompanied by the words "The Truth Is Out There." It was from their favorite show. Every week Tariq would record *The X-Files* and bring the tape over to Matt's house. They'd watch it in his basement, geeking out accordingly. Obviously, Matt thought this t-shirt was pretty cool. So cool, in fact, he owned the exact same shirt. The problem was they were currently both wearing it.

"Why are you wearing that shirt?" Matt asked.

"I don't know. I just am," Tariq said.

"Shit. We need to coordinate this better. We can't be wearing the same exact shirt. We look like retarded twins."

"It's not that big a deal."

"We look like idiots. Next time you plan on wearing that shirt, call me the night before to make sure *I'm* not wearing *my* shirt."

There was nothing Matt could do about this now. Luckily it was the end of the day and the first time they'd been seen together. Thank God. What an embarrassment it would have been had they walked down the hallway in matching *X-Files* attire. People would have started calling them Mulder and Scully, and with Matt's luck, he'd be Scully.

"Crazy about Kurt, right?" Matt decided to address the topic of the day. He couldn't remember if Tariq was a fan or not.

"Yeah." Along with a solemn head nod, this was the only response Tariq gave. Maybe he wasn't a fan? He then reached into his backpack and pulled out a box of condoms. He handed them to Matt. "They were eight bucks."

Matt looked embarrassed and motioned for Tariq to hold them lower.

"Jesus. Could you be more subtle, it's embarrassing."

"Why?" Tariq questioned.

Good point. Buying condoms meant you were planning to have sex. What's embarrassing about that? That's awesome. For some reason Matt had been too embarrassed to buy condoms. That's not entirely why he told Tariq to buy them for him, though. Since Matt didn't have a car and couldn't exactly ask his mom to take him to a pharmacy, Tariq agreed to make the purchase.

"Eight bucks? Fuck that's expensive," Matt complained. Tariq just shrugged his shoulders as Matt pulled out a crumpled five-dollar bill from his pocket. "All I have is a five. I owe you the rest."

Tariq took the money without voicing any objection. Matt actually had another five in his pocket, but assumed Tariq wouldn't have the two dollars in change. It was easier this way.

"You're going to use those tonight?" Tariq asked.

"That's the plan. I'm almost done here so I figure if you could just drop me off right after school, that'd be great. I want to have time to relax, clean up the basement before Rebecca comes over to watch a movie." Matt made air quotes as he said "watch a movie."

'I can't."

"What do you mean?"

"I can't. My mother needed the car today so I took the bus."

Matt started to panic. "How the hell am I supposed to get home?"

"Take the bus," Tariq said.

"The bus?" Matt was insulted by the suggestion. "I haven't taken the bus since ninth grade. No way."

"I don't know," Tariq said. "Maybe Jeff can drive you. Or someone over at Seth's."

Matt couldn't hide his contempt. Why didn't Tariq warn him about this sooner? For the past three years Matt had managed to get rides from friends or his parents. With three months left in his high school career there was no way he was going back to taking a school bus. Matt needed to get home fast, but it looked like he'd first be making an unscheduled stop at Seth's house.

Jeff

"...so I do understand how you guys feel today. The Beatles meant everything to me as a teenager and then for John to just be gone like that. It felt so senseless. So evil. Here was a man who was all about peace and love. And because of him, my whole generation felt that those qualities were the most important things about life. I still believe peace and love will trump everything else. He gave my generation hope. A voice. My then-boyfriend and I went down to our local pub, and everyone there, old, young, black, white, we just started singing 'all we are saying, is give peace a chance.' It went on for hours. I needed that community, that collective sense of loss to help get through the pain I was feeling. I know so many of you need that today. You lost someone important to you. I want you to know, you're not alone. We've all felt this pain and confusion at some point in our lives. It's important to talk about it. To make sure it doesn't lead us to do something rash. So rather than talk about elements and scientific formulas, I thought we could just talk about Kurt Cobain and what he meant to all of you."

Jeff Rosenduft watched as his chemistry teacher, Mrs. Heller, delivered this sentiment. She was pulling out all the stops, even sitting on her desk to appear more relatable. She was clearly worried all the students were suddenly going to start committing suicide. Jeff was as big a Nirvana fan as there could be, but even he found that a preposterous notion. Just because Kurt Cobain killed himself didn't mean everyone who loved him would. This man was a soulful genius and an artistic inspiration, but he was also just a musician. This wasn't a Jim Jones or Waco situation. There were no hidden instruction buried deep inside a track on *In Utero* telling teenagers to kill themselves.

Who knows? Maybe there was someone out there unhappy with their life and seeing Kurt take this step to end his inner pain would give them ideas. Jeff was relatively happy with his life, so it was hard for him to understand. He never had to deal with real pain. Jeff was never seriously ill or in a tragic accident. He'd never lost a loved one; in fact, his great-grandparents on his mother's side were still alive and well, married for seventy-five years. In the fall he was going to the college of his choice, the School of Visual Arts in Manhattan, to study film. Even his beloved New York Yankees were looking to have their first playoff-bound season since he was a toddler. Life for Jeff was still worth living.

Mrs. Heller cared enough to cancel the scheduled test and just sit around and talk about what was on everyone's mind. She cared enough that she wanted to make sure no one killed themselves. However, her comparison about John Lennon felt false. John Lennon was murdered. That meant there was someone to blame. The anger and confusion Mrs. Heller had felt could be directed at Mark David Chapman. Who would Jeff direct it at? The logical person would be Kurt himself. After all, he was responsible for his own actions. Why couldn't he keep it together? Why couldn't he stay clean? It felt wrong to put the blame at Kurt's feet though. He was a victim too. A victim of addiction, fame and his own mind. As Mrs. Heller went on about grief, Jeff suddenly started to get annoyed. Because whatever frustration, whatever feelings Jeff was starting to have about Kurt Cobain would have to wait. Today something more important was happening. Today he was going to ask out Katie Keating!

...maybe.

Katie worked at Hot Topic, the store in the mall that specialized in mass-produced unique alternative culture. Jeff worked at Movieland, the video store next door. After seeing Katie at a Freaks show, the two realized they knew each other from eating in the mall's food court. After that, almost every day they took their breaks together. Jeff used to always bring his food, but didn't want to look cheap in front of Katie, so he stopped. Panda Express, Taco Bell, Wendy's— considering he only made minimum wage this was costing Jeff a fortune. But he didn't care what his bank account looked like. It was a good excuse to spend time with a smart, beautifully odd girl.

Katie had an unassuming face and a body that was usually hidden behind a t-shirt and jeans combination, but she had an attitude that made her desired by all who met her. That attitude was first noticed in her messy, matted hair, which she changed the color of on a frequent basis. Last time Jeff saw her it was Manic Panic red. She also was self-deprecating to a brave degree. Never afraid to admit she was the one who farted or that in a certain light you might notice her slight mustache. On the side of her beat-up Oldsmobile she painted gaudy flames, which looked ridiculous but only made her love the decision to paint them even more. She was the kind of girl who would come into work wearing makeup that made it look like she had a black eye, and would spend the day telling every customer a different story about how it happened, ranging from "I fell in the food court and I'm now involved in a lawsuit against the mall" to "I just got out of an abusive relationship." Whereas most teenagers didn't have a sense of pop culture past, Katie loved old TV shows and often talked about wanting to get a tattoo of Grandpa Munster. Currently the only tattoo she did have were three X's on the inside of her lower lip. XXX signified she was straight edge and refrained from using alcohol, tobacco or drugs. Jeff didn't think of himself in this way but considering he also didn't drink, smoke or do drugs, he assumed he was by default "straight edge" too. The most attractive thing for Jeff, however, was Katie's artistic abilities. She liked to make buttons and shirts with funny images or sayings on them.

After Katie discovered that she and Jeff shared the same favorite horror film, *The Shining*, she made him a large button in which she replaced Jack Nicholson's face menacingly breaking through the doorway, with Jeff's face. How had she done this? The work was seamless. And she just made this for him out of pure kindness. Out of the fact that it was something Jeff simply might like.

When Jeff first met Katie she was dating a guy from her school named Dennis. Almost immediately into their friendship, Katie confessed to Jeff her desire to end the relationship. It's hard to dump someone and she didn't want to hurt him. So for weeks Jeff listened every day to her going back and forth on the matter, never telling her to end things outright but always encouraging her to do what was best. He knew he couldn't be perceived as trying to break them up if he was ever going to ask her out himself. One week ago, Katie came into Movieland and told Jeff she had ended things with Dennis. Jeff's heart soared. The girl he'd been pining for the past few months was finally available.

So now what? Could he just ask her out? Was it that simple? Jeff began to second-guess himself. He didn't want to make his move too fast, it might appear insensitive. That said, Katie was a hot commodity. He'd already heard the lead singer of Macaroni & Shit made his move by writing her a song. And one of the Hodrinsky twins had mentioned his excitement at the news she was single. Sure, Kurt Cobain was dead, but Jeff had to push down all those emotions until he figured out what to do about the Katie situation.

Jeff had dated a few girls here and there but none of the relationships ever seemed to stick. Mostly it'd be a girl who was new to video class. Usually a sophomore. She'd be impressed with some film he made, they'd go out a few times to the movies or mini golf, fool around and then she'd move on. It's not that they didn't like Jeff, because every single one of them remained friends. Jeff assumed they simply thought they could do better. Maybe they were right. There was always someone smarter, funnier and more handsome around the corner. After all, if Jeff was so great, why wouldn't any of these girls stick around? Pathetically, his most meaningful relationship had lasted only eighteen days and they didn't even have sex. To make things more confusing, he still considered Jackie Spampinato to be his best friend.

Being alone hurt. Exciting things were happening for Jeff and he wanted someone to share them with. What good was happiness if you had to experience it alone? He wanted someone to take to prom. Not as a friend but as someone he could kiss out on the dance floor. He knew this was a cheesy thought, the kind his friends like Nick and T.J. would mock. Who cares if they mock him? There's a sweetness to prom, to being there with someone you love, that Jeff totally bought into. Once Jackie asked him if he had to pick between being the next Steven Spielberg or finding the love of his life, which would he choose. Without hesitation Jeff said love. That's what's most important. He often wondered if that meant he didn't really have the drive to make it in the film business. You have to be brutal! You have to choose your art over people to make it! That's silly. How can you have great art without knowing love? When Jeff thought about how much he wanted love, he'd cry. Jeff cried at a lot of things. At very very sad or very very happy films. At stupid feel-good news stories about elderly couples who had been together for seventy-five years. At Danny Elfman's haunting score to *Edward Scissorhands*, which he had taken to falling asleep to every night, his pillow wet with tears. Mostly Jeff cried about his own loneliness and strong desire to find love. It was the one thing he wanted and he couldn't have it. It hurt so much. Every day.

Maybe Jeff had real pain inside him after all?

"So," Mrs. Heller said. "Does anyone want to talk about what they're feeling?"

*****

Ninth period for Jeff was usually devoted to finishing up some video project. Today it was devoted to wandering the halls aimlessly. He was in a daze, wondering what to do when he saw Katie later. Everyone probably thought he was in this state because of the tragic news. That might be for the best, otherwise he would have to explain himself. Jeff had a history of romanticizing women, making them the only thing that mattered. Every girl who even smiled at him, he started to imagine a future together. Not just the immediate prom future but a real future. Marriage. Kids. This only made the pain worse when he was inevitably rejected. He was crazy and he knew it. You're just a high school senior. Why are you thinking about this?

Jeff was on his way over to Seth's. Hopefully Nick LeWinter would be there. Nick knew how women's minds worked. He knew just how much pressure to apply in any given situation. Nick knew if you needed to come on strong or calmly hang back. Since that was Jeff's question about Katie, Nick was the man to ask. Granted Nick's goal was sex and Jeff's was a relationship, but he assumed the advice would translate.

Jeff found himself passing through the commons where Jackie was struggling with a vending machine. It wasn't like her to cut. She had the best GPA of anyone Jeff hung out with. A perfect student, except of course for her unfair reputation. Before Katie was the love of Jeff's life, Jackie was. Jackie was considered the most non-traditionally beautiful, beautiful girl in the school, which basically meant she wasn't a cheerleader and liked to get high with dirtbags. It wasn't her looks that made Jeff love her. It wasn't her brain either. It was that she didn't give a damn. Every day she walked around with a screw you attitude towards anyone who tried to knock her down. Behind her back they'd call her a slut or whore. T.J. even implied this at the diner one night, causing him and Jeff to get into the only fight they ever had. In the boys' bathroom, someone wrote on the stall door she was a cum-dumpster. Hypocrites. Jeff liked having sex. Was he a whore? Jackie did things every boy would do in a heartbeat. The implication of this also confused Jeff. Did all the boys want to be with a virgin? Jeff hoped he'd never be in a situation where he had to take a girl's virginity. When he lost his virginity to Amy Slotnick, a friend from his Jewish day camp days, he was thankful she knew what she was doing. It put Jeff at ease that his first time was with an experienced friend. Someone he trusted. They did it a few times over the course of two months, but Amy didn't want any more than that. She liked Jeff enough to give it a try, but not to be in a relationship.

After her "incident," Jeff saw an opportunity with Jackie. At first he worried he'd be taking advantage of her by finally making his move when she was at her lowest. But he decided there's no better time to let someone know they are loved than when they're at their lowest. One day after school, Jeff found Jackie alone out by the handball courts, where only days earlier cruel graffiti was removed. It looked like she'd been crying. They'd been friends for a few years, her always dating some jerk and Jeff always too scared to make an actual move. He told her he knew the timing wasn't perfect but that he was in love with her. That the reason he loved her was because she didn't care what people thought. That she may feel broken by what people were saying, but he knew how strong she was. At the end of the day she'd tell them all "screw you" and stand taller than everyone. And on that day he wanted to be by her side. Not only as a friend, but as more than that. Then Jeff told her the first time he saw her, he thought she was quite possibly the most beautiful woman he had ever seen. With the adrenalin flowing from this confession, Jeff made by far the boldest romantic move he'd ever made. Before Jackie could respond, he grabbed her, pulled her close to him, and kissed her. To his shock, she kissed him back. The next eighteen days were the most glorious of his life. And then it was over.

He still carried a small torch for Jackie. They remained friends because his love for her was beyond romantic and quite frankly she needed all the friends she could get. Jeff would never abandon someone who meant this much to him. It was hard to watch her screw around with other guys, especially guys Jeff knew. It was even harder when a few months ago she started dating some college idiot who wouldn't even show her the respect she deserved by meeting her friends. Jeff didn't like the way she was being treated but he could only object so much because Jackie saw all of his complaints as jealousy. She wasn't off base. There was probably thirty percent jealousy involved. However, that meant there was seventy percent caring friendship.

But now there was Katie. The first girl he'd met who made him feel all those things Jackie once did. Jeff didn't want to ask Jackie for her advice about the Katie situation. It was still weird, probably because of that lingering thirty percent. Would it ever go away?

Jeff walked over to the vending machine, bought Jackie a Coke and suggested they head over to Seth's, together.

T.J.

It was probably the nicest home of all T.J.'s friends. Isolated at the end of a cul-de-sac, it stood out from the other rich cookie-cutter houses on the block. First off, it was on a small hill, elevating it ever so slightly from the rest of the neighborhood. This alone was enough to make it the envy of Wheelwright Way. Secondly, rather than grey or brown vinyl paneling, the Feldmans had made the bold choice of going with blue. Mr. Feldman had also converted the basement into his own personal playhouse, equipped with everything a man suffering from a mid-life crisis would need. Pool table, Ms. Pac-Man arcade game, big screen television and a fully loaded bar. The backyard was huge. In-ground pool, a trampoline and a killer grill which the Feldmans used frequently. Both Mr. and Mrs. Feldman worked for MetLife. They were mucky-mucks of some sort, T.J. could never remember, nor cared what their exact job titles were. He just knew that they were generous with their money and they made a lot of it.

But none of this was why T.J. liked the house.

Outside his friend Seth Feldman's bedroom window was a flat rooftop above the garage. Whenever Seth would throw a "garage party," T.J. liked to stand on this rooftop, scream at the top of his lungs, and wildly hurl himself off of it into the bushes below. Jeopardizing his body like that would cause cheers from all the attendees. Usually they demanded he do it again, and he'd always accommodate. This was his party trick. He didn't even have to be drunk or high to be convinced to do it. In fact he worried intoxication might cause him to slip up and seriously hurt himself. Not that throwing yourself off a garage roof into bushes didn't hurt.

So far people hadn't grown tired of this stunt. T.J. was terrified of the day they would. When everyone goes off to college will they still find causing physical harm to oneself funny? Would T.J. be throwing himself off roofs for all eternity while Jeff Rosenduft, Jackie Spampinato and all the other friends he grew up with became successful?

Seth Feldman's parents would allow him to throw wild parties all the time, the logic being he'd be safer partying under their roof than in a gutter somewhere. They'd let him book bands to play in the garage. The Freaks, darlings of the Long Island ska scene, played their first show in Seth's garage. His parties were the thing of local legend. And all Seth had to do to get his parents to be so accommodating was be a recovering heroin addict who tried to kill himself.

The other reason everyone loved Seth's house was that it was one block away from the high school and always open to anyone who wanted to stop by. And every day after school students of all types would just walk in and head up to Seth's room to have a beer, smoke a bowl or just listen to music. Despite the proximity, Seth didn't go to Smithtown High School. After his parents found him passed out in the garage, the engine of the family's minivan running, they had placed him in a rehab center. When he got out they were worried about sending him back to school, mostly because of how the community would react to a student on methadone. If only they knew how much more fucked up the student body really was.

Every morning Seth had a tutor come and teach him what he'd need to know to pass his Regents exams. By the afternoon he was always free to hang and his parents would encourage the open-door policy, knowing Seth needed to maintain some sort of social life. They even knew he smoked pot, but chose to look the other way.

Despite being big supporters of the D.A.R.E. program, they were liberal enough to realize no one ever OD'd on weed.

"Happiness in Slavery" blared from the home, filling the neighborhood with an energy that juxtaposed the setting. T.J. was still young enough that something like that amused him. Entering the house, he noticed the lighting fixture above his head shaking. The whole ceiling shook. Seth was stomping around his room, gaining some sort of manic energy from Trent Reznor's voice.

T.J. climbed the stairs, approaching Seth's room. Would they talk about Kurt Cobain? Do you bring up suicide to someone who tried to kill themselves? But if T.J. didn't bring it up, that would be weirder. It would be offensive; the idea Seth couldn't handle hearing about suicide. It was obviously something that had to be brought up immediately.

All 6'4, 250 pounds of Seth Feldman thrashed around his bedroom. Sweat pouring beneath his messy green hair down his chubby face, he didn't even notice T.J. walk in until he blurted out, "Did you hear about Kurt Cobain?"

"It's cause he's 27," Seth shouted back, over the music.

"What's that got to do with anything?" T.J. questioned.

"All great musicians die at 27." Seth paused his dancing and lit a cigarette as he finished his point. "Jimi Hendrix. Jim Morrison. Um, Janis Joplin."

"Really? Where'd you hear that?"

"It's a thing, just a thing, you know, that people know."

Suddenly a tiny voice T.J. had not realized was in the room with them spoke up. "My dad loves Janis Joplin. He's got a nude picture of her hanging in our living room."

The voice belonged to a small, thin girl wearing a pink sweater three sizes too big for her. Her hair was short, blonde and choppy, as if she, or more likely Seth, had taken scissors to it haphazardly. Her features were pointy and she looked like a cute dinosaur. T.J. was attracted to her instantly.

"Oh shit, do you know Liz?" Seth overexcitedly said. "How come I never thought to introduce you two? Fuck! You two should know each other. Liz goes to Commack."

Commack was two towns over, but T.J. immediately knew that's not how Seth met her. She had her oversized sleeves rolled up, exposing her pale arm. Dozens of healed scars. Was she just a cutter or did she try and kill herself as well? Maybe he shouldn't have brought up Kurt. No, that's ridiculous. It's the biggest news of the day, possibly of their lifetime. Anyway, T.J. was still dumb enough about life that the cuts she had inflicted on herself only made him more attracted to her.

"Should we be listening to Nirvana?" Seth said manically. "I mean is it fucking disrespectful if we don't?"

"You were gonna show me that movie," Liz begged sweetly.

"What movie?" asked T.J.

For the next twenty minutes Seth was rummaging through a crate of unmarked, dusty VHS tapes. He kept popping them in hoping it'd be the right one. *Beavis and Butthead*. Nope. *El Mariachi*. Wrong. Finally he found it. The footage was black and white, and bad tracking made for a grainy image, but the actions were unmistakable. A dirty toilet flushed and the camera followed waste down through a series of pipes. After a minutes-long journey the end of the pipes was reached. It was connected to a person tied down in a rubber suit, the filthy water pouring into their mouth. Although no feces were shown, T.J. remained convinced he saw shit. This was the Nine Inch Nails' *Broken Movie*.

"Is this real?" Liz said.

"Yeah! I bought it from a guy in a parking lot after a show," Seth answered.

This sadistic tape had already reached something of mythological proportions. You couldn't buy it in a store or order it through the mail. You had to know someone who knew someone who could make you a copy. The quality of each copy of a copy was worse than the last, only adding to the mystique. It was strange and upsetting. T.J. sat riveted as a bald man sat in a room full of flies while eating a steak. Occasionally a fly would go into his mouth and he would eat it as well. This couldn't be real, could it? How would they fake eating flies? Trent Reznor is the kind of man who *would* know a guy who willingly eats flies. Fuck, if Trent asked T.J. to eat flies or dog shit, he'd do it too.

What made watching this brutal but rare video more special was that he was doing it while sitting next to a pretty girl. The only thing that could make this even more special would be to get stoned with a pretty girl.

"Seth, can we smoke from The Creeper?"

Seth smiled at T.J.'s suggestion. From under his bed, he pulled out two very long PVC pipes and started to put them together. This was a giant bong he had built and dubbed The Creeper. He only liked to smoke from it on special occasions. Like the day Kurt

Cobain died. Or the day they watched *The Broken Movie* with a pretty dinosaur.

"I'm gonna piss." With that Liz stood up and left the room.

"You should fuck her," said Seth. This was at least confirmation for T.J. that Seth wasn't trying to fuck her. Seth never really seemed interested in sex. On more than one occasion he said that he had no use for it. T.J. assumed this was just talk. Everyone has use for sex, especially those who aren't getting any. It was probably the drugs or lack thereof that killed Seth's sex drive. That said, when he wanted to get off, Seth would have sex with anyone. He was open about being bisexual. Two years back he dated a hot Goth girl named Kat, who later got chlamydia. Seth would also be quick to tell stories about some hot emo guy he went down on at the rehab clinic. One night while the two of them were getting stoned, Seth had offered to give T.J. head. At first T.J. said yes. He figured they were close friends and it would just be an experience they could share. He'd even gotten as far as taking his semi-erect penis out of his pants, before he chickened out.

"You think she'd be into me?" T.J. sheepishly asked.

"Fuck yeah! I want this to happen. I don't know why I didn't think of you two before!"

"She's really cute. She reminds me of a velociraptor."

"Right!? You two should fucking date and have babies. I *love* this match. Here's what I'm gonna do. I'm gonna let you borrow my car. Go drive around with her. Bring her to The Freaks show tonight! Or isn't Sage having a party? Yes, bring her to Sage's party and fuck her! Fuck her in that shed in the backyard."

T.J. liked this idea. Not the fucking her part per se; Seth's insistence on them "fucking" was starting to sound crass (although if she wanted to he wouldn't say no). Instead he liked the idea of driving around and getting to know her. It'd been awhile since he'd gotten to know any new girls.

"Maybe," T.J. answered.

Liz strolled back into the room with a smile on her face, just as T.J. and Seth took their first hit from The Creeper.

"I know how I know you," she said. "You kicked that guy in the head at Seth's last party. Then you threw yourself off the roof."

T.J. was sure he had thrown himself off the roof but didn't remember kicking someone in the head. Liz continued.

"Yeah, you were sitting by the pool, and there was a dude passed out on the front lawn. Seth wanted him gone and you stood up and said, 'Seth, you let me get drunk and stoned at your home, I will do anything for you' and ran into the front yard and kicked the guy in the back of the head!"

"Oh shit, I did that?"

"Yeah. The dude shot up and started wandering into the street holding the back of his head. It was hilarious."

They laughed, smiling at one another.

*****

When you meet someone new, time stands still. And that's exactly what happened for T.J. He and Liz were watching *The Broken Movie* for the second time. Her body would scrunch up into his every time she was repulsed by the images on screen, and he'd smile with hope and excitement for the evening ahead. Time also stands still when you're very high, and T.J. was very high. Liz had chosen not to smoke. T.J. offered twice just to be friendly but wasn't going to push it. In his seventeen years no one had ever pressured him to do drugs, even though in middle school all his teachers assured him someone would. Obviously he wasn't going to become this cliché towards Liz, even though there was no way she didn't have a contact high.

T.J. had been so lost in the weed and the film and Liz that he hadn't noticed that the room had filled up. The school day must have finally been over. On the bed, flipping through a *Details* magazine, was Nick LeWinter. Nick was the keyboardist for The Freaks and as always he was dressed in a dirty blazer. T.J. knew him for two things: One, the fact that he rarely bathed, and two, he attributed this lack of hygiene for his ability to pick up women. Nick felt ladies were drawn in by his natural male musk, but T.J. figured they were into him because he was part of a popular ska band. It couldn't be because of his looks, since he resembled the love child of Howard Stern and a Fraggle.

Standing over Nick was Jeff Rosenduft. How had T.J. not noticed Jeff was in the room? They had been friends since grade school, and even though they didn't dress alike, take the same classes or listen to the same music, they remained close. Jeff stayed more straitlaced, didn't drink, didn't do drugs, but liked to hang out with people who did. Dip a toe in dangerous waters.

"Hey Jeff!" T.J. said.

Now it was Jeff who became startled by T.J.'s presence.

"Hey T.J."

T.J. only now started eavesdropping on what Jeff was saying. Something about that girl at Hot Topic he was into. Jeff was asking Nick for advice and motioned for him to leave the room for a private chat. This wasn't going to end well.

Jeff and Nick remained silent as they navigated the minefield that was Seth's floor, trying carefully to avoid stepping on T.J., Liz, a dozen unlabeled VHS tapes and The Creeper. They were unsuccessful. Jeff's foot came down on one of the cassettes, cracking it. Worried, Jeff looked over at Seth, but the big guy waved it off without a care. After all, the most important tape he owned was already playing in the VCR.

Finally the pair exited, squeezing past a girl who was blocking the doorway. Jackie Spampinato was now in the room. T.J. made an active decision to ignore her, mostly because Jackie was easily the hottest girl he had ever seen. She was the hottest girl most of them had ever seen, and T.J. often wondered why she would spend so much time with a bunch of assholes. Jackie was wearing a frilly black skirt and tall black boots. In between there was six inches of exposed skin. Forget asses or tits, T.J. felt this was the sexiest part of a woman. That area from lower thigh to below the knee. It was a beautiful tease of what lay under that skirt. Normally it would drive T.J. insane just to think about it. Today, however, he had more pressing matters. He was trying to make something happen with Liz. So he wouldn't even give Jackie a further glance.

Unfortunately, there was one other person who now awkwardly stumbled into the room. He practically tripped over his own feet, accidently kicking the cracked tape, sending it sliding into T.J. and hitting him in the leg. T.J. looked down at the VHS and then glared at Matt Pace. Matt was harmless enough but rubbed T.J. the wrong way. Something about him always felt phony. Matt was the kind of person who tried way too hard. But *all* were welcomed at Seth's.

"Crazy about Kurt, right?" Matt said.

"I guess," answered Seth. "I mean, I'm not *that* surprised."

T.J. decided it was time to get involved in the conversation, if only to annoy Matt.

"Fuck him. His music sucked anyway."

This declaration got a giggle out of Liz. Who cares if it was because of a contact high, T.J. wanted to keep it going.

"What are you talking about?" Jackie chimed in. "He's a genius."

"*Was*," T.J. reminded her.

This got another laugh out of Liz. Let's keep going, he thought.

"His music defined our generation," Jackie protested.

"It didn't define me."

"Nirvana is our Beatles."

"The Beatles suck too."

This got the biggest laugh yet. Jackie turned to Liz. She seemed shocked by having to defend this point and even more shocked she was being laughed at.

"What's wrong with you? A man is dead." Disgust oozed from Jackie's voice.

BEEP BEEP BEEP

Jackie's beeper went off, saving T.J. and Liz from further scorn.

"I need to use your phone." With that Jackie left the room and headed downstairs.

"Can anyone give me a ride home?" Matt asked.

No one ever wanted to give Matt a ride home, and yet every day this task would fall to someone. Why did they put up with this? T.J. also didn't have a car, so he couldn't belittle Matt for bumming a ride, although he wanted to.

"Jeff would," Matt continued, "but he has work and it's in the complete opposite direction. Are any of you guys able to?

No one answered so Matt kept talking.

"Ugh, it's just I have to get home before my girlfriend comes over."

"Bullshit!" T.J. blurted out.

"That I have a girlfriend?"

What T.J. wanted to say was, you can't have a girlfriend because I don't have a girlfriend. But he didn't want to look desperate in front of Liz.

"Where'd you meet?" T.J. asked.

"At a show. Her name is Rebecca. She's from Dix Hills."

An audible "oh" came from everyone left in the room. Dix Hills was a rich town known for their upstanding Jewish princesses.

"You nail this J.A.P. yet?" T.J. asked in an interrogating tone. This was the question on everyone's mind so it might as well be asked.

"I will tonight. Which is why I have to get home!"

"So you're going to lose your virginity tonight to a girl from Dix Hills."

"That's the plan," Matt said with pride.

"You're a virgin?" Liz asked.

Before Matt could answer, T.J. cut him off. "Of course he is. Has this chick at least blown you yet?"

T.J. was being cruel for no reason. Wait, that wasn't true. He was being cruel for a really good reason. He didn't like Matt. He didn't like hearing about Matt's girlfriend. And as an added bonus, he wanted to look strong in front of Liz.

"No, Rebecca hasn't blown me yet."

"Get her to blow you. Jewish girls give the best head," T.J. said.

"Is that true?" Matt asked with a twinge of excitement in his voice.

"Yes," Seth answered. "At least according to any of the guys I've blown."

T.J. had wanted to keep pushing Matt about this girl, but unfortunately Seth had defused the situation. Not only that, he'd gotten the biggest laugh out of Liz yet.

Jeff

"Nick, can I talk to you for a minute?"

Jeff had just entered Seth's room. It was more crowded than usual. Besides Nick and Jackie, Seth was stomping around to Nine Inch Nails while T.J. and some cute girl Jeff didn't know were watching *The Broken Movie*.

"What's up?" Nick answered without even looking in Jeff's direction. His head was buried in a *Details* magazine, the Spring Fashion Issue featuring Ethan Hawke. Jeff often wondered if Nick was considered fashionable. He always wore a blazer, which made him look more adult, but it was a ratty blazer, stained with vomit and smelling like the men's room at Penn Station. Is this what looks good? Jeff had just transitioned to wearing his spring attire, switching from Yankees sweatshirts to Yankees t-shirts. He had no fashion sense and wondered if that's why women didn't stay with him.

"Do you have a minute?" Jeff asked again. "Can we talk outside?"

"Hey Jeff!" T.J. suddenly shouted, startling him. He was so focused on getting Nick's attention he forgot T.J. was sitting at his feet.

"Nick," Jeff continued, "Hot Topic."

Nick finally looked up, smiled and closed the magazine. A private conversation about a girl. Jeff had piqued his interest. Nick closed the magazine and climbed off the bed. Jackie was blocking the doorway, her body language saying she didn't really want to be here. As they squeezed past her, Jeff noticed Nick give Jackie a

40

quick up and down. Jackie noticed too, a slight smile creeping across her face. Did they sometimes still fool around?

Jeff had briefly considered asking T.J. to join them too. After all, he was closest with T.J. and there was no questioning his loyalty as a friend. Once, at a show, someone for no reason called Jeff a "short piece of shit." Without hesitation T.J. punched the guy in the throat, sending the jerk to his knees. And this wasn't some scrawny emo kid, this was a big dude. Far bigger than T.J. Football player big. T.J. didn't care what the consequences might be. Didn't care that he could get arrested or beaten half to death. He was an in-the-moment kind of guy. Jeff admired that. It's the thing he admired most about his punk friends. They just didn't give a damn. How liberating must that be? To have no worries about grades or expectations. To not care about ripping your clothes, getting a black eye or knocking out a tooth. T.J. did this trick where he'd throw himself off the roof of Seth's house and never get hurt. For all Jeff knew, if he threw himself off the roof he wouldn't get hurt either. Who would ever think to try it the first time? Jeff worried about everything. It's why he was the only one of his friends with an after-school job. It's why he didn't drink or smoke. There were consequences to life that T.J. didn't care about. While Jeff was going off to college, trapped by conformity, T.J. would keep living life the way he wanted to live it. Raging against the machine. Jeff wished he could channel his own rage, but he didn't even curse. He'd like to think he had a little bit of dirtbag in him because of the company he kept, but at the end of the day he worried he was just a tourist. Just painfully average. He could visit Seth's house and go to punk shows, but would he ever truly be accepted? Only loyal T.J. would be by his side, ready to punch anyone in the throat who dared question him. Did T.J. even realize how revered he was?

But no, Jeff opted to keep this conversation between him and Nick. This was the only man for the job, and as much as Jeff valued T.J.'s friendship, girls were not his specialty. So off to the hallway they went, Jeff hoping for some sage-like wisdom.

"What do you need?" Nick asked. "Something about Katie?"

"I don't know if you heard, but she's back on the market," Jeff said.

"Really? I hadn't." Nick seemed very surprised by this development. Was it because Katie was single or because he didn't know about it? "So she finally broke up with what's his name. It's about time."

"Right," Jeff continued. "And as you know, I've developed certain feelings for her and I'm not exactly sure how to proceed."

"Just ask her out. You guys have gotten close. She has to see this coming," Nick said.

"But I don't want—"

Nick gave Jeff a head nod, signaling someone was coming up behind them.

"Hey Jeff."

It was Matt Pace. Jeff found Matt likable enough but understood why he annoyed so many people. What he liked best about him was that Matt was the only person at school who knew as much about films as he did. And he was talented. Maybe more talented than Jeff. Jeff wished he could tell a narrative story like Matt could. Instead he would just run around, trying to capture real life. It felt lazy, unfocused and unplanned. He got into art school, but was it really art? Why wasn't Matt going to a real film school? Why was he settling for a SUNY school?

"Hey Matt, what's up?"

Jeff knew he was going to ask for a ride home.

"Could you bring me home?" Matt asked.

Jeff gave some excuse about not having time to bring him home before work. It was only half true. If Jeff left right now he could take Matt home with time to spare, plus even if he was late, his boss, Vic, wouldn't really care. Jeff wanted to finish his conversation though. It was far more important than work or helping a friend. If Matt didn't have a ride, why didn't he just take the damn bus? Still, he wished he could have helped.

Nick made no excuse. He barely looked Matt in the eye. It was clear he wasn't going to help and Matt wasn't going to ask. Jeff wished he could be more like Nick.

Matt headed into Seth's room, and Jeff continued.

"I want something with Katie. I want something real. So I don't want to mess it up by moving too soon while she's down. That's what I did with Jackie and I'm convinced that's why it didn't work out."

"That's not why it didn't work out with Jackie. Jackie is fucking nuts."

Jeff grimaced at Nick's comment.

"I haven't been able to make any relationships stick," Jeff said. "I want a girlfriend for more than just eighteen days. I really like this girl."

Nick seemed to think long and hard about what to do. "The problem with waiting is, you'll be friend-zoned. Shit, you might already be friend-zoned."

"What does that mean?" Jeff asked.

"The friend zone. It's when you're already too close of friends for anything romantic to happen. You're like a brother. You've been giving her all this carefully thought out brotherly advice about her relationship, right? I hate to be the bearer of bad news, but it might be hard for her to see you as anything other than a friend."

Uh-oh, was Jeff stuck in the "friend zone?"

"However," Nick continued, "I know you don't want to just fuck this girl. You want her to fall in love with you. And you're right, if you want love you need to give her space."

"See, that's what I thought," Jeff exclaimed, feeling validated. "It's so hard when there's someone you want so badly to not just tell them."

"I get that. Has she given you any signs she might be interested?" Nick asked.

"She made me a button." From his pocket, Jeff pulled out his *Shining* button. He carried it with him everywhere. Nick studied it.

"That's cute. She makes funny shit." Again Nick paused to think. "It's not hopeless."

"She's a hot commodity. Guys are already hitting on her," Jeff said.

"And she rejected them?" Nick questioned.

"So far. I can't tell if it's that she needs space or if—this sounds so egotistical—or if maybe she's waiting for me to ask her out. I don't know, that's crazy."

"It's not crazy," Nick assured him. "Give her time. Be the last man standing. The next person who gets with her will never get a fair chance unless they give it time. Trust me."

This sucked. Jeff wanted to march into Hot Topic today and tell Katie how he felt. However, breakups are hard, even if you're the one doing the breaking. She needed time.

"Thanks, Nick. This is why I came to you. You know women."

"Hey, when you've been with as many as I have, you pick up a few tricks. Listen, I gotta get out of here and meet up with the band."

"Cool. I'll see you at the show," Jeff said.

Nick smiled, headed down the stairs and out the door. This was the smart play. Jeff just needed a friend to confirm it.

Jackie

Everyone was watching some disgusting video that looked like a snuff film. Was it *Faces of Death*? All Jackie knew was that it was scored by Nine Inch Nails. The second they arrived in Seth's bedroom, Jeff made a beeline towards Nick LeWinter and was picking his brain about a girl. That's a dumb idea. Just because Nick gets laid all the time by treating girls like shit doesn't make him an authority on how to seduce women. At least not women anyone would really want. Jackie understood why Jeff might feel awkward asking her for advice, considering she was pretty sure he still, on some level, wanted her.

Jeff asked Nick to leave the room for a more private discussion. This left Jackie alone with a group of stoned punks. T.J. Weber, Seth Feldman and some weird girl that looked like a bird. At that moment Matt Pace stumbled in. Jackie liked Matt. Sure, he talked too much (in fact before he was fully in the room he'd already mentioned Kurt Cobain), but he talked too much because he really wanted to be part of things. He really wanted to connect with people and was just awkward at it. So he yammered on until he got a response. Matt was also one of the few friends who hadn't ever overtly hit on her. Jackie realized he'd been in the room only .03 seconds and was already eyeballing her body up and down; but he couldn't help himself. He wasn't being rude. Matt was just a high school boy, and that's why Jackie was now dating a college man.

It didn't take long for Jackie to find herself in another argument over the merits of Nirvana. T.J. was talking shit and Jackie didn't want to hear it. Something about today and this topic in particular had brought out a rare combative streak in her. She should spar with people more often.

"The Beatles suck too," T.J. shouted with a laugh.

The statement lacked all logic. This wasn't an argument Jackie could win. T.J. was just baiting her for kicks. Being a contrarian. There are some things that are just fact. The world is round, gravity exists and The Beatles are great. Even if you didn't love The Beatles you had to consider them great by the sheer force of how they changed art, music and the world. Jackie didn't remember when she first learned this fact because it was knowledge you're just born with. Fuck T.J.

"What's wrong with you? A man is dead." This was the only retort she could think of and it wasn't even about The Beatles. If combativeness was going to be a trait she embraced, she might need to take a debate class.

It aggravated her even more because she and T.J. used to be close. Over the last year she noticed him getting angrier and angrier. Was it his perpetually sick mother? Was it the dissolving of his relationship with Maureen? Jackie remembered thinking she needed to talk to him, to try and find a way to help. Then one night he made some shitty comment about how she should blow him for a Belgian waffle. The insensitive prick probably didn't even remember saying it. She could have confronted T.J. Instead she shut down and shut him out. Not the mature thing to do, but she had to worry about her own teenage miseries. Would the brand-new argumentative Jackie be so passive aggressive? Hell, maybe she'd finally confront T.J. on why they're no longer friends.

BEEP BEEP BEEP

Saved by technology. This time Sean's page did require a response. Jackie left the room, left this stupid discussion and went downstairs to use the kitchen phone. She could hear them upstairs, laughing at her, as she dialed Sean's number. The other end began to ring. Jackie pulled a cigarette from her bag, the first cigarette of the afternoon, and lit it. The phone kept ringing. If he wanted her to call him back, why wasn't he picking up? Jackie had some ideas. Turning on the faucet, she put a small amount of water in a plastic cup and ashed in it.

"Hello." Finally, Sean answered.

"You paged?"

"Hey babe. Just wanted to see what the plan was? What time you coming on by?"

"I can head over now."

"...Awesome." He hesitated. Why would he hesitate? Again, Jackie had ideas. "So maybe we can order a pizza and have a few beers, watch a flick," Sean said.

"Tonight is that show in Huntington," Jackie said. "And then that party at my friend Sage's. Everyone's going to be there and I want you to meet them."

"Come on babe, you're above all that high school party nonsense. You're already dating a college *man*. Let's just hang in the dorm tonight. You and me."

"I know they're just lame high school kids but they're my friends. And in a few months I won't be able to see them anymore. That's why I want to go to the party," she said.

"Why don't you come by and we'll talk it out." Sean was going to try and convince her to stay in. He'd order a pizza from the college commissary, they'd have a few beers, smoke a little pot, he'd put on some of that awful jam band music he listened to while she blew him, afterwards he'd finger her for a bit while waiting for his dick to get hard again, they'd fuck, then he'd put on some pretentious independent film and they'd fall asleep while watching it. This was their routine. Jackie couldn't remember the last time they'd left the Stony Brook campus together. Maybe only once or twice, and that was just to rent a movie or go on a beer run. Tonight Jackie was determined to stand her ground. They were going out. If he was such a "man" he'd take her to a show, buy her dinner and meet up with her friends.

"I'll be over in about thirty minutes."

"Later, babe."

Jackie hung up the phone and dropped what was left of her cigarette into the cup.

"Sounds like you're not coming to the party." Jeff's voice startled her. How long had he been standing there?

"Jesus Christ, stop sneaking up on me today."

"You've dated this guy for three months and none of us have met him? Are you embarrassed to bring your sophisticated boyfriend around 'lame high school kids'?" Clearly Jeff had been there long enough.

"I didn't mean that."

"So *he's* embarrassed to be around 'lame high school kids.'"

"Nobody is embarrassed," she said. "He's coming to the show and you'll get to meet and ridicule him in person."

"Look, I want to like him but I don't like that he keeps you locked away."

"Did you ever think I might want to be locked away? You think I'm a kept woman?"

"That's what people think."

"When have you ever known me to give a fuck what people think?"

"I care about you and I'm worried about you, that's all. Sean Greco seems like bad news. I mean he's in college and dating a high school girl. That's a red flag."

"You're just jealous."

"No, no, no." This set Jeff off. "I've dated plenty of girls since you. Two years ago, maybe even a year ago, yeah, I'd be jealous if you decided to date some jerk just because he doesn't have any connection to your past, especially when there are perfectly nice guys right here who love you. But now, I'm just making sure my friend isn't being taken advantage of." Jeff headed out the door. "I can't wait to meet him."

Jackie resented the fact her friends felt she was being taken advantage of. She knew who Sean was and what this relationship was. She also hated the idea she should be with a nice guy. The idea that someone got to be with her just because he opened car doors, paid for a Coke at the vending machine or didn't overtly try and sleep with her, made Jackie sick. It was a turn-on when someone hit on her. Why would she want some passive asshole who waited around jerking off when she could be with a guy who wanted her so bad he came right out and said it?

The accusation of jealousy was a bit of a low blow. Jackie knew Jeff was probably just concerned for her as a friend. She also assumed there was still part of him that wanted her and always would. In fact, as late as January she'd heard through the grapevine

Jeff referred to her as "the one that got away." Again, the implication that he caused her to leave rather than her *choosing* to leave.

In May of their sophomore year Jackie and Jeff dated for exactly eighteen days. Yet for the next year of his life Jeff compared every girl he met to her. It was flattering. In those eighteen days they never did more than make out. Jeff never tried to do anything else and to this day he's the only guy Jackie dated that she hadn't slept with. At the time he was a virgin, and Jackie didn't want the responsibility of changing that. He was obsessed with her and she wasn't into him nearly enough to reciprocate that obsession. Going further would have only hurt him. She'd actually tried to feel something more for Jeff but just wasn't attracted to him. Not that Jeff wasn't an attractive guy. He was just kind of plain. Nondescript. Not Jackie's type. There had been an incident at school a month before, one that would define Jackie's high school life. The kind of incident that would still be discussed at their twentieth reunion. "Hey, remember what happened to Jackie Spampinato in sophomore year?" "Jackie Spampinato, queen of the whores? How could I forget?" After the incident, Jackie decided she should go for the nice guy and that nice guy was Jeff. She actually wondered if Jeff only asked her out because she was damaged goods. At her lowest point who else would want her? She came to realize Jeff was genuinely in love with her, had in fact pined for years. So she gave him eighteen glorious days before deciding this nice guy thing wasn't for her.

Matt

Jeff was huddled in the corner of Seth Feldman's second floor hallway, talking to Nick LeWinter. Matt didn't want to interrupt them, it looked like a serious conversation, but he also knew Jeff was his best shot at a ride home.

"Hey Jeff," Matt said.

Jeff looked up, distracted. What were he and Nick talking about anyway? Hopefully it wasn't advice about a girl. Even Matt, a virgin who had never had a steady girlfriend, knew better than to do that.

"Hey Matt, what's up?"

"Could you bring me home?"

"I can't," Jeff said. "I've got a four-hour shift at the video store I'm already going to be late for."

"You can't drop me off on the way?" Matt was pushing it. Jeff's job was in the complete opposite direction.

"Sorry. You live in the complete opposite direction." Jeff was trying to be nice and not blow Matt off, but it was obvious he wanted to. For his part Nick said nothing. He wouldn't even make eye contact with him. Despite that, Matt started to open his mouth to ask, before deciding against it.

Not having a car is probably the worst thing that could happen to a high school senior. Matt felt he should be done with a life of bumming rides off friends and acquaintances. It seemed like everyone he knew had something to drive. Most classmates' parents used their children's coming of driving age as an excuse to buy something new, giving their old car to their kids. Or they were hand-me-downs from grandparents who no longer were able to drive. In the case of Tariq, he shared a car with his mother, a woman who rarely left her house. Matt knew how to drive. He'd taken the test using his father's car and got a perfect score. What was the point of having a license with nothing to drive? It was embarrassing when his mom would drop him off at Rock N Bowl on Friday nights. Or there was a time recently when he was meeting Jeff and Jackie at the Smithtown Movie Theater to see *Reality Bites*. After having to beg his mom to drop him off, she finally agreed. Then, to his horror, she got curious about the film and decided to see it for herself. Matt couldn't enjoy any of the Gen-X turmoil on screen knowing his mom was sitting only a few rows back from him and his friends. Humiliating.

Matt was convinced that not having a car adversely affected his sex life, too. He couldn't pick a girl up to take her out. He couldn't meet her anywhere. Why even bother asking a girl out under these circumstances? He'd be asking her to drive him. And if she didn't have a car, well, it'd be over before it even started. That's why this girl he'd been seeing was such a miracle. Rebecca had a car and didn't seem to care that Matt didn't. Still, he couldn't call her and say, come pick me up after school, like he was her fucking child. He needed to get home where she was coming over to "watch a movie."

As he peered into Seth's room, Matt took note of who else was there that could possibly drive him. Jackie might, but she'd been so aloof lately who knows what she's liable to say. T.J. didn't have a car either, a fact that seemed to bother him a lot less than it bothered Matt. In fact T.J. not being bothered about this sometimes bothered Matt more than not having a car. Seth had a car but it might be weird to ask him to leave his own home to drive him. There was some weird girl, who kind of looked like an unattractive version of Laura Dern, sitting on the floor, enthralled by the Nine Inch Nails' *Broken Movie*. Did she have a car?

Matt was nervous. He assumed none of these people would be willing to help. Lost in his anxiety, he stumbled into Seth's room, practically tripping over a VHS tape which for some reason was on the floor. The tape went sliding into T.J., hitting him in the leg. It couldn't have hurt, but from the glare T.J. shot him, Matt knew it had annoyed. Somehow it seemed worse to simply annoy T.J. than to hurt him. Now more than ever, better to break the ice before asking this group for favors.

"Crazy about Kurt, right?"

That was a mistake. Somehow he'd opened the floodgates. Jackie and T.J. were now arguing about the merits of Nirvana. Before Matt even had a chance to ask her for a ride, she was out the door, responding to a page, no doubt from her absentee college boyfriend.

"Can anyone give me a ride home?"

This opened up *another* can of worms. Now Matt was getting grilled about his love life and getting some good-natured, but kind of annoying, ribbing from T.J. about how Jewish girls give good head. Matt would have to just ride it out. That's the price for not having a car.

"So…is anyone going to drive me?" Matt finally asked again.

"I don't even have a car. You know that," T.J. coldly replied.

"I don't either. And, I don't even know you," the strange girl said with a giggle.

This left only Seth as Matt's final prayer for a lift.

"T.J.," Seth said, "give the boy a ride." Seth tossed T.J. his keys.

T.J. clearly didn't want to. He made a not-so-subtle gesture towards the girl. Seth gave him a pretty obvious "so what" look back.

"Liz," T.J. said, "you wanna hit the kitchen and grab a snack before we go?"

"After watching this," she said, gesturing towards *The Broken Movie*, "I don't know if I'll eat for a week."

The pair got up and headed downstairs. Success!

Matt was now left alone with Seth. All 250 pounds of him slowly started walking towards Matt, huge grin plastered across his face. Seth threw an arm around him. He was dripping with sweat and it was getting all over Matt. Now Matt was going to smell like some bisexual heroin addict. He was going to have to add shower to the list of things to do before Rebecca's arrival.

"So," Seth said, "you're gonna fuck for the first time." He said this with a real sense of pride in his voice. Seth saw himself as some sort of guru who loved getting involved in his friends' love lives. To be fair, he always seemed to want what was best for them, but Matt couldn't help think there was a creepy ulterior motive. Every Seth party felt like a desperate attempt at trying to start an orgy. He'd set up special rooms for people to fuck in, rather uncreatively called "Fuck Rooms." Matt was old-fashioned and thought the idea of screwing someone in front of your friends was weird. Maybe that's only because he'd never had sex before. After tonight, who knows, he might be up for a world of new and perverse experiences.

"Yeah. I'm pretty sure tonight it's finally going to happen," Matt said, beaming.

"Do you like this Rebecca?"

"I do."

"Not just because she's willing to fuck you, right? Because I can get a girl to just fuck you, you know." If that was the case why hadn't Seth done that in the past? And what the hell was he asking?

"No. She seems really cool," Matt said.

"How many time have you gone out?"

"Three. We hung out at the diner one night. Went to play mini golf another. And last week we saw *The Mighty Ducks* sequel."

"How was it?"

"Terrible. Its kid's stuff, but we both liked the first one and nothing else was playing. She seems to like movies, so I invited her over to watch one tonight."

"But you don't plan on watching a movie." Seth's huge smile somehow got wider.

"Not even for a minute." Matt smiled back. Suddenly Seth's face turned serious and his grip around Matt tightened.

"Are you nervous?" Seth asked.

"No. Not at all." Matt was actually very nervous. Who wouldn't be their first time? He knew Rebecca wasn't a virgin, but he hadn't told her he was. In fact when discussing exes, he alluded to at least one sexual encounter he'd had with a girl last year on a cruise ship. Not only was this cruise ship girl made up but his family had never even been on a cruise. So Matt was *very* concerned he'd be terrible at sex.

"You're going to be terrible at sex." Seth told Matt this, devoid of any humor in his voice.

"Well...I mean...I...."

"No. It's going to be weird and you're not going to be good at it. It's not like in all those movies you watch. You might not fit inside her easily. There'll be a lot of awkward moving around, trying to find a comfortable angle. And it'll be over really fast. Like, before you know it fast. My first time I was so excited, I came while putting on the condom. Just be honest and generous and it'll work out. By the third time you fuck her, I'm sure you'll get the hang of it."

T.J.

"That video was swiss!"

T.J. stared at Liz, confused as to what "swiss" meant. Should he ask?

They were now alone in the kitchen, leaning back against the counter, eating Sunny Doodles. Seth's parents always had the best snacks, too.

"What's swiss?"

"Oh, when Seth and I met at, you know, *the place*, we started coming up with new slang. Like new words to use," Liz said.

"Swiss means cool?" T.J. asked.

"Yeah! Or like if it's a hot chick you might call her a swiss Betty. Or a cool dude would be Swiss Swistofferson."

"You're a swiss Betty." The second these words came out of T.J's mouth, he regretted them. He wanted to compliment her, but it would've be weird to tell her she looked like a sexy dinosaur. Swiss Betty sounded so phony coming out of his mouth.

Liz just smiled politely. To offset the awkwardness T.J. lit himself a cigarette. He gestured the pack towards her. She declined.

"So does it hurt when you throw yourself off a roof?" Liz asked.

T.J. thought about it.

"I mean it doesn't *not* hurt. But I know what I'm doing."

T.J. had no idea what he was doing when he threw himself off rooftops. Or when he would go down into the sewer. Or climb up onto the water tower at night. He liked to pretend he knew what he was doing. That he knew the right way to fall. The fact was, he just did it and so far hadn't gotten hurt. Could he make money off of this? If he wasn't going to be a high school graduate maybe he could be some sort of stuntman or part of the Jim Rose Circus. He needed to get this "act" on video.

"Could you teach me?" Liz said, a little too excited.

"Um—"

"I have a really high pain threshold. So if I fell wrong it wouldn't hurt me too much. And I don't mind scars. I have all kinds of scars. Look!"

Liz lifted up her sweater and exposed a burn scar on her soft white belly.

"When I was little my father was cooking soup in a giant iron kettle, and it exploded. I got burned really bad. I used to be embarrassed by it but I'm learning to accept that my flaws actually make me special."

This raised so many questions. Why was her father cooking with an iron kettle? Why was Liz shirtless around it? And most of all, what kind of soup was it? T.J. was about to ask when Matt came bounding into the room.

"All right ramblers, let's get ramblin'."

Matt said this with a shit-eating grin on his face. T.J didn't want to drive Matt, but it was Seth's car. And Seth wanted T.J. to take Matt home to lose his virginity.

T.J. didn't say a word. Instead he reached back into the box of Sunny Doodles. He ripped open the packaging and shoved an entire cream-filled golden cupcake into his mouth. Then he handed the second cake to Liz, who did exactly the same. Some cream oozed out the side of her tiny mouth. T.J. desperately wanted to lick it off her face but Liz wiped it clean with her sleeve before he even got the chance to pretend he'd make such a bold move.

The three of them stared at each other in silence. The world's stupidest Mexican standoff.

"Are we going? I've got places to be, people to do," Matt said.

T.J. grabbed the box of Sunny Doodles and led the way out the door.

The car ride was going to be ten minutes at most but would feel like eternity. T.J. just wanted to talk to Liz. He hadn't even asked if she wanted to spend the rest of the night hanging out with him. For all he knew she was going to have to go after this. Instead he had to listen to Matt, droning on and on about sex. Sex, a topic Matt knew nothing about. The longer they spoke about it, would T.J. be exposed as not knowing much either?

"I bought condoms," Matt said. "Man, they're expensive. Love should be free, am I right?"

"You can get them free at Planned Parenthood. That's what I do," Liz replied. She then proceeded to pull a fistful of multicolored prophylactics out of her bag.

"Whoa, you must do a lot of fucking!" Matt exclaimed.

This crassness was the final straw. T.J. popped in one of Seth's mixtapes and cranked KMFDM's "A Drug Against War" at full blast.

Matt got the idea, finally shutting up. T.J. decided to head-bang and thrash in his seat until they reached their destination. For her part, Liz cracked open another Sunny Doodle.

Seth's tiny, beat-up Honda pulled into Matt's driveway. T.J. had to step out and pull the seat forward to let Matt squeeze through.

"Thanks for the ride. I owe you one."

As T.J. watched Matt walk up towards his house, the wheels began turning in his head.

"Liz," T.J. said. "Hand me those Sunny Doodles."

Box in hand, T.J. pulled out a cupcake. Those years of being forced to play Little League with Jeff finally paid off. He reared back and fired a perfect strike into the back of Matt's head. The Sunny Doodle exploded, filling Matt's hair with cream. Liz shrieked and clapped with delight.

"What the fuck?!?" Matt turned around just as T.J. fired another. This time he ducked and the cupcake hit the front door. Gooey cake slowly slid down to the ground, leaving a trail of cream.

"Stop it!"

But T.J. was far from done. He fired two at the garage door. Three more at the windows. The box was now empty and Matt's house was a mess.

"Asshole!" Matt screamed. He'd have to clean all this up and Rebecca would be here any minute. At this realization, a smile crept across T.J.'s face that said "good."

T.J. jumped back in the car and sped out of the driveway, Liz cackling the entire time. Once they turned the corner, he pulled over.

"The look...the look on his face. It...it was so...*sad*." Liz was laughing so hard she could barely get the words out.

"Hey," T.J. interrupted. "You wanna hang tonight? There's this show in Huntington and then this party at my friend Sage's."

"I don't feel like going to a show."

T.J's heart sank.

"But," she continued, "if you bring me to seves, I'll let you buy me a Slurpee."

Matt

Seth had gotten into Matt's head. Was that supposed to be some sort of pep talk? Matt understood the reality of the situation. Another thing on his to-do list before Rebecca arrived was masturbate. That might help him last longer, but still, the second he felt the real thing it'd basically be game over. Maybe if he thought about movies? *Schindler's List* perhaps.

As T.J. and Liz reluctantly drove him home, he was trying not to panic. It was getting closer and closer to the time he'd no longer be a virgin and it was hard to think of anything else. So in true Matt Pace fashion, he began to ramble on about it. What was he saying about condoms? Why did he basically just call this Liz girl a slut? Matt knew he talked non-stop. Silence made him uncomfortable. It made him feel bored and lonely. What's the point of being around people if you're not going to interact with them? And once he felt that, out came a slew of verbal diarrhea. Couple that with his nerves, he just couldn't help himself. It wasn't a trait he was proud of, but just because you're aware you do something annoying doesn't mean you can stop doing it. T.J. cranked up the music, a clear sign Matt should be quiet. An industrial sound blared from the speakers. Matt assumed the band they were listening to was KMFDM only because they kept shouting their name insistently throughout the song.

Rebecca Padover wasn't just going to be the first girl Matt had sex with. She was the first girl he'd even kissed. He'd told Seth they met at a show. This was a lie. The truth was Rebecca was a set-up. By their parents. How could Matt possibly tell guys like T.J. and Seth that without being laughed at? The only one who knew the truth was Tariq, and only because Matt had to tell somebody. Rebecca's mom used to go to the same synagogue as

Matt's, and one day they were talking about how their children should meet. Matt's mom was probably already writing down the names of grandchildren before she even suggested this set-up. At first Matt was against it. It's weird having your mother play matchmaker. Who wants their mom involved in their sex life? But then he saw a picture of her. She was gorgeous. Entirely out of his league. Beautiful olive skin, long curly brown hair and what sealed the deal for him, giant breasts. Matt was no expert but they were probably 36 double Ds.

Matt was really into girls with Semitic good looks. What was it about SGLs that turned him on so much? The big breasts were a clear factor. There was also something that Matt found attractive about larger noses. It made a girl stand out from the crowd. A year ago a sophomore named Leah in his video yearbook class was always complaining about how big her nose was and that she couldn't wait until she was eighteen to get it fixed. This disgusted Matt. Her nose was perfect. It fit her face just right. What she found ugly actually made her pretty. Matt told her that if she got a nose job, it would probably fuck up her face. She'd look boring like everyone else. Then he asked her out. She said no.

The real reason Matt was attracted to SGLs more than any other type of girl probably was rooted in some deep psychological meaning involving his Jewish mother and her Judaism always being forced to take a backseat to his father's Catholicism. He tried not to think about this because, again, it involved his mother in his sex life. Besides, despite celebrating the holidays of both religions, Matt was pretty confident there was no God.

Jewish girls were his ideal, looks-wise, but Matt believed beggars can't be choosers. He was attracted to all sorts of women from all walks of life. He'd asked out an Aryan goddess from his Spanish class. An Asian skateboarder from Photography. A

Columbian girl that at first he thought was Asian, from a Freaks show. Matt didn't know any black girls his own age but he'd recently had a very vivid sex dream featuring all four members of En Vogue, so he assumed he was open to that as well. Matt was just attracted to women he found attractive. And which women did he find attractive? Most.

But Rebecca was beautiful by all standards with which you could describe beauty. And somehow Matt was dating her. Their first date was meeting for a bite at the Millennium Diner. They discussed how embarrassing their moms were for doing this, complained about their schools and talked about what their hopes for college were. She was planning to study mental health and social work at Hofstra. He confessed his lack of a car and she was nice enough to drive him home.

Their second date was miniature golf. During the back nine he kept thinking he should find a time to kiss her. It was around the windmill he had his best chance. He was helping her line up her shot, standing behind her, both of them gripping the club. It was a move he'd seen in a movie. He predictably chickened out. On their way to her car, he knew he had to try. He'd never kissed anyone before, but how hard could it be? Millions of people do it every day. Suddenly, he stopped her. He warned Rebecca, in a very neurotic fashion, that he was going to kiss her. Something else he'd seen in a movie. She didn't stop him. The kiss was everything he wanted it to be. An exciting new experience that made his heart soar. Even thinking about it now gave him goosebumps. Rebecca didn't know it was his first kiss and he felt it hadn't come off that way.

The third date, he held her hand all through the movie. It was everything he ever wanted, except maybe for them to be watching a better movie. Afterwards they had a conversation about past relationships. Rebecca had dated a few guys but nothing had stuck. She admitted to being sexually active with almost all of them. What was Matt supposed to do? Tell her he'd been rejected by every girl he'd ever been interested in? He'd look like a loser. Instead he talked about making out with a few girls at parties, never meeting the right person. Admit to never having a girlfriend but lie about actually touching women. Then came the story about the girl on the cruise ship. It made sense to him. Two teenagers meet on a boat full of adults for five days, of course they'd end up fooling around. It was a lie that felt reasonable. Admit to being sexually inexperienced but not a virgin. Rebecca seemed to buy it. Storytelling, after all, was Matt's expertise.

Now Rebecca was coming over. It was her idea, suggested after they made out in her car at the end of their third date. "Why don't I come by Friday and you can show me one of those movies you're always talking about?" Matt knew that movie equaled sex.

Finally they pulled into the driveway of Matt's house. He stared at his home. Typical suburban Long Island. Nothing special about it. Would Rebecca think it was below her? After all, she was from Dix Hills. Nah, she wasn't like that. If material things were important, she'd be dating a guy with a car.

T.J. stepped out and pulled the seat forward. Matt struggled to squeeze through, momentarily getting tangled in the seatbelt. T.J. didn't seem to notice. He was completely fixated on this new Liz girl.

"Thanks for the ride. I owe you one."

Matt headed up his driveway. A spring in his step. Rebecca would be here in an hour. It was all he could think about....

SPLAT!

Something hit Matt in the back of the head. It felt sticky. He reached back into his hair. Cream filling. Matt turned around to see T.J. firing a Sunny Doodle right at him. Using reflexes he didn't even know he had, Matt dodged it. T.J. wasn't done. He kept firing them at the house. Bam! Bam! Bam! Sunny Doodles exploded on the garage, the windows, the front door. Liz cackled like a psycho.

"Asshole!" Matt screamed.

T.J. leaped back into Seth's car and peeled out of the driveway. Maybe Matt should have taken the bus home.

*****

There was no time to clean up the mess of Crappy Doodles all over the front of the house. Technically there might have been time, but Matt had a decision to make. He could either spend it taking a shower, jerking off and setting the proper romantic mood in the basement or he could waste it peeling cupcake wrappers off the windows. The choice was obvious.

Matt had just finished using a damp towel to wipe the back of his head when his father came home from work.

"What the hell happened to the house?"

This was declared to no one in particular. Matt walked out into the hallway to see his dad standing there, looking more confused than angry.

"It's just a prank my friends pulled," Matt said.

"Your friends did that? The front of the house is covered in…what is that?"

"Sunny Doodles," Matt answered. "And it's not 'covered.' It's just in a few spots. I'll clean it later. Or in the morning."

"In the morning?" His father sounded more outraged now. "You can't leave that overnight. It'll attract animals. Raccoons and opossums."

The clock was ticking.

"Dad, Rebecca is going to be here in less than an hour. I wanted to shower before she arrives."

"Then you'd better get out there and get started," his father demanded.

Why was Matt's dad being so unreasonable? Hadn't he noticed his son never brought women around? This was a big deal. A big fucking deal.

"I don't want to be out there cleaning up Crappy Doodles when my girlfriend shows up. It's embarrassing." Matt's voice was starting to crack. He was getting upset.

"I don't want the side of my house covered in shit. Your idiot friends did this, it's your responsibility to clean it up."

"Please dad," Matt was getting red-faced. "Can you do it for me?"

"No."

"Dad," he was starting to raise his voice. "I don't want her to show up while I'm doing this! I'll have to explain it!"

"Explain what?"

"THAT MY FRIENDS THREW CUPCAKES AT ME! IT'S FUCKING EMBARRASSING!" Matt was having a fit, the kind toddlers have, and his father didn't care for it.

"Calm down. You're not a child. What if your girlfriend saw you like this? Huh? I don't care what you tell her. Make something up. But you're cleaning up those Crappy Doodles, now!"

Matt didn't know what to do. His father was right about one thing. If Matt didn't calm down it could blow things with Rebecca. There wouldn't be enough time to shower and prepare; hopefully he just wouldn't be caught mid-cupcake cleanup. Matt headed outside.

"There's a bucket and sponge in the garage," his father said, adding insult to injury.

Moments later, Matt found himself filling up the bucket with water and heading towards the porch to wipe down the front door. The issue wasn't the amount of Crappy Doodles, it was that T.J. had gotten them in some hard-to-reach places. Was there really one stuck to a second-floor window? Fuck. Matt headed back into the garage to get the ladder. Either the ladder was unwieldy or Matt was weaker than he thought, because he had a hell of a time dragging it into the front lawn. Great, Rebecca would probably arrive just in time to see Matt couldn't even lift a ladder. What did she see in him? Other than a vast knowledge of film, he wasn't very smart. At least school-wise, that is. Matt knew he wasn't ugly but he also knew he wasn't handsome. Had he been, it wouldn't have taken him seventeen years to lose his virginity. He gathered Rebecca was being pressured into only dating other Jews. It sounded like many of her past boyfriends weren't and this fact was slowly killing her grandparents. Matt was half Jewish so that seemed like a good compromise between her and her family.

Matt finally got the ladder in place, climbed up and began washing the windows. The cream was tougher to get off than he thought, especially on glass. Dirty water spilled onto his X-Files t-shirt. Then he climbed back down, looking for the next cupcake.

There was one, right in the middle of a driveway. He started to peel the wrapper off the ground just as a BMW pulled up in front of his home. Had it already been an hour? Was Rebecca early? Matt watched as the car door opened and out stepped a goddess. Her curly hair flipped as she turned. A bright white smile beamed across her face. She was wearing a tight black shirt, with a zipper that only stretched from her neckline to her chest. These kinds of shirts drove Matt wild. She was zipped up now, but he loved the idea that with a quick motion he'd get an eyeful of cleavage. It was enough to momentarily distract Matt from the humiliating task at hand.

Rebecca strutted up the driveway towards him. It was then that Matt realized how stupid he looked.

"Hey," she said, "what's that?"

"Oh, it's, ugh…"

"Is that a cupcake wrapper?"

"Yeah." Matt was going to have to explain this. He hadn't thought up a story. "My idiot friend T.J. drove me home and as I was getting out of the car he started pegging me with Crappy Doodles. And they got all over the house. He's such a fucking dick. Then my dad was like, clean them up now! It just got me so angry. I wanted to wash up before you got here but instead I look like a retard cleaning cream filling off my driveway."

Matt had rambled the truth. Had he come off really whiny while doing so? He just couldn't stop himself. Rebecca seemed unfazed. She put her arms around him and gave him a short but meaningful kiss on the lips.

"Do you need help?" she sweetly asked.

"No, I think that was the last one." He was surprised this scene didn't bother her. Maybe it wasn't a big deal after all. Maybe Matt had made a mountain out of a molehill. "Let's go inside," he continued.

Rebecca took his wet hand as they headed towards the front door. He decided to forget about putting the ladder away.

"Crazy about Kurt, right?" Matt added as they walked inside.

*****

"Think about it. A mulatto. An albino. These people are outsiders. Kurt was an outsider. Teenagers are outsiders."

Matt had just gone on about Kurt Cobain for fifteen minutes, impressive considering he hardly knew anything about him. It was the topic of the day and he assumed Rebecca would want to discuss it. She hadn't contributed much, though. Just a few comments about how sad it was that someone would kill themselves. She couldn't comprehend things being so bad in your life that'd you'd feel the need to end it, especially if you were a million-dollar recording artist.

"So," Rebecca said, trying to change the subject, "what movie are we going to watch?"

They were sitting on a comfy brown couch in Matt's wood-paneled basement. This is where he spent most of his free time. His parents never came down here so they let him set up a TV and two VCRs. He used these VCRs to make copies of every film he could get his hands on. He'd go to Blockbuster Video to rent a movie, take it home and play it on one VCR, while using the other VCR to record it onto a blank VHS tape. This is why Matt's VHS collection was the best of anyone he knew, even Jeff. An entire wall of the basement was devoted to these tapes. It towered over them; stacks of tapes with the names of films hand-written on the spine in black Sharpie marker. Everything from *Citizen Kane* to *Star Wars*. *Psycho* to *Apocalypse Now*. Matt would copy them even before knowing if he'd like them. That's why he owned so many dull Oscar winners like *Gandhi* and *Out of Africa*. There were few things in this world he was more proud of than this collection.

"Is there a film you always wanted to see? Because I have everything."

Rebecca gazed up at the wall, clearly intimidated by having to make this decision. "What's your favorite movie of all time?"

Matt was about to blurt out *A Clockwork Orange*. It was the first film he saw where he realized movies weren't just entertainment, that they could deliver complex ideas in original ways. After seeing it, he devoured all of Kubrick's work. But he wasn't going to suggest they watch an old movie full of rape on their fourth date. He decided to go with the film he'd been most recently inspired by.

"*Reservoir Dogs*."

"Oh, I've heard that's good."

"You haven't seen it?" he asked with excitement.

"No. I'd imagine you've seen it a lot though."

"Like a hundred times, but I'm always happy to watch it again."

Reservoir Dogs had been playing in the background of Matt's life for the past year. He loved how stripped-down a story it was. Just eight guys, nine if you count the cop, and a heist gone wrong.

It felt like something he could make. This time, however, he had no intention of actually watching the movie. Shit, she's never seen it. Matt should have suggested something he knew Rebecca had already watched before. Like *Ferris Bueller* or *Back to the Future*. He didn't want her to miss out on a great film. Maybe they'd wait until after the movie to fool around.

Matt grabbed his copy off the shelf and put it in the VCR.

"Do you have any snacks?" she asked. "Popcorn? Oh, what about some of those Sunny Doodles!"

Matt stopped dead in his tracks. "Why would you ask if I had Sunny Doodles?"

"I don't know. Your friend was throwing them so I thought maybe there was a box somewhere."

Matt's whole body language had changed. He slumped down and his face turned to stone.

"He's *not* my friend."

"Well, you called him a friend so I assumed—"

"He's just this asshole who's friends with my friends," Matt fired back curtly.

Rebecca didn't seem quite sure how to handle this. She tried to backtrack.

"Well, I'm not that hungry. Maybe after the movie we can go to the diner. Or Friendly's and get ice cream."

Matt realized she was trying to move on and continue the evening in a positive manner, but now he was obsessing over the Crappy Doodles again and how pathetic he must have looked.

"It's just, I was really embarrassed when you got here. And now you bring them up again. I want to move on from it."

"O.k." Rebecca was trying to address him in a calm, caring tone. She waved him over to the couch. "I didn't mean to embarrass you."

Matt sat down next to her. She threw her arms around him and he pressed play on the remote.

*****

It was still early on in the film. The part where we learn Mr. White's backstory. Rebecca seemed to be enjoying it enough. The opening sequence talking about tipping and Madonna produced a few genuine chuckles out of her. It would have been nice if they hadn't used the word "virgin" so much. Stop projecting. As far as Rebecca knew, Matt once fucked a girl on a cruise ship.

During the next twenty minutes, Matt noticed Rebecca getting closer and closer to him. When the movie started they just sat quietly beside each other. Minutes later she was holding his hand. Minutes after that she was leaning up against him. Now she was lying on him, her head in his lap. Her fingers danced across his legs. Matt was starting to get hard. She must have known this too—after all, her head was next to his crotch.

Despite Matt's body telling him what he wanted, suddenly his head was filled with doubt. Seth was right, he was going to be awful at this. How could he, a boy who'd only just recently kissed a girl, please a woman like this? It will be humiliating.

Rebecca gazed up at Matt. He felt her eyes on him. Instead of looking, though, he stayed focused on Harvey Keitel.

Humiliation. Why had T.J. tried to humiliate him by throwing all those Crappy Doodles? Who gets off on making others feel like shit? Everything that had happened in the last few hours made Matt feel like less of a man. The inability to drive himself home, having Tariq buy condoms for him, Seth, T.J., his father. Shouldn't this painfully beautiful woman, who was now sliding her body up against his, make him finally feel like a man? Why wasn't this working?

Rebecca was now face to face with Matt. Straddling him. Is she not enjoying the film? He claimed it to be his favorite movie. Shouldn't she be respectful of something this important to him?

"I want you," she seductively said.

"I just want to watch the movie," was his cold reply.

With that Matt physically pushed her off of him and slumped into the couch. Sulking. Matt had never seen a more shocked and disgusted look on another human being's face than the look on Rebecca's. Why had he done this? Why was he suddenly rejecting this gorgeous SGL?

Now it was Rebecca's turn to feel embarrassed. After a few moments of confusion, it became clear she was not going to take this. Matt couldn't blame her. There wasn't another man in America who would have rejected her in that moment. She began to gather her things. Could he stop this? Could he course-correct and apologize? It doesn't have to be over. But he just couldn't. Something inside wouldn't allow him to say anything. Wouldn't let him explain the thoughts that he barely understood himself. What's wrong? Stop her from leaving.

Without saying a word, Rebecca headed upstairs and out of the house. Matt watched *Reservoir Dogs* alone for a few more minutes before hitting stop on the remote.

Jackie

Jackie's little red Hyundai hatchback sped down Route 25A towards the Stony Brook campus. She wasn't going to Sean's dorm empty-handed. She came bearing a gift. All last night Jackie had been working on a mixtape. Sean was constantly sharing his favorite music with her and she hated all of it. It was repetitive, endless hippie nonsense. If Jackie had to listen to one more bootleg from a Phish show or some rare Grateful Dead recording, she'd kill herself. At first she gave these bands a fair chance, but no matter how stoned she got, the music only produced apathy. What Jackie hated the most was how Sean believed this music was made specifically for him. You can listen to every Grateful Dead song ever written and smoke all the pot in the world, but it won't suddenly mean you're from the 1970s. Sean acted like this music was from his era. As if he understood what it was like to be at Woodstock. He came of age in the 80's. His favorite music should be The Smiths, The Cure, or Prince. It's one thing to enjoy a song from, say, the 1950's, but it's another thing to act like it's your music. That you're going out every night to drink milkshakes and attend a sock hop. You should lean into *your* generation. So Jackie had been up until 2AM making him a mixtape reflecting the music that inspired her. Music made for this generation by people who understood this generation. And in Jackie's case that meant an all-female mix.

Tori Amos started it off. "Cornflake Girl." Tori was Jackie's newest inspiration, and her latest album *Under the Pink* played in her car constantly. Tori Amos had overcome personal tragedy through her art. Jackie believed she was a goddamn hero and aimed to be as strong as her. She followed that up with some Björk, The Cranberries and Ani DiFranco. Jackie briefly debated if she should include Mazzy Star. Would it slow down the mix too much? Fuck it, she had to. "Fade into You" always made her swoon. She hoped it would have at least a fraction of that effect on Sean. After that she ratcheted up the rock. L7, The Breeders and a Kim Deal-led track by The Pixies, "Gigantic," a song about a black man with a big penis. Jackie wanted to include The Pixies because she'd heard Sean reference them but wasn't convinced he actually knew who they were. Finally, in an attempt to hold on to nothing as fast as she could, Jackie ended the mix with more Tori, "A Pretty Good Year."

But it was track three that for Jackie made the whole tape. Sean's reaction to it would forever color her opinion of him. Jackie's favorite song of all time. One that spoke to her in ways nothing else could. Liz Phair's "Fuck and Run." The song is about a girl who wants a boyfriend but ends up in one-night stands with guys who are decidedly not interested in anything more than fucking and running. However, there's some confliction in the song and this is what made it Jackie's personal anthem. Does Liz really want a boyfriend? Or does she also enjoy the seeming immaturity of the fuck and run cycle? A big part of Jackie felt she deserved all that stupid old shit like letters and sodas. But a bigger part of her felt like a modern woman who does what she wants without caring about the old-fashioned crap society tells her she deserves. She felt this way forever, even when she was twelve, but it wasn't until hearing Liz Phair put it into words that she understood. Jackie was allowed to be a hypocrite about love and sex. When she began dating she thought you needed to have a boyfriend who you can devote yourself to. And every relationship she began, no matter how small, started off with the hope they would be worthy of that devotion. Eventually the guy would either use her just for the sex or she'd spend too much time trying to make a round peg like Jeff stick in a square hole.

What Jackie liked about her relationship with Sean was that she knew where it stood. At most, this could never last beyond the summer. Rather than go into a relationship with hope for a future, Jackie went into this one assuming it would end with a fuck and run. If Jackie wanted to have adult relationships she'd have to learn to be a realist about these things. Sean was a training ground. A man outside her world whom she didn't have to worry about hurting or being hurt by.

Then why was she making him a mixtape full of emotionally meaningful songs? Why was she so upset he didn't want to meet her friends? Why was she bothered by the fact she was 99% sure he was cheating on her? He was probably escorting some slut out of his dorm room at this very moment. Jackie wanted to fuck. Jackie wanted to run. Jackie wanted to have a boyfriend. Jackie wanted to be won over because goddammit she deserved it! And Jackie wanted to just be left alone. She felt this all simultaneously. It was beyond confusing, which is why she could never explain it to Jeff or any of her friends. The only person who understood was Liz Phair.

*****

Walking through the cluttered hallways of the dorms always made Jackie feel a bit like an imposter. She enjoyed the feeling though. An outsider. It meant if she did something stupid they couldn't hold it against her. After all, she didn't really belong here.

Reaching Sean's door, Jackie was about to barge in. But you can't just assume he has a girl in there. Don't be rude, knock. Then she heard the strumming of a guitar from inside. It was probably all clear, and she should do a knock/barge combo, opening the door while knocking.

Jackie cracked open the door to find Sean, slumped into his favorite chair, a beanbag chair, guitar in hand.

"Babe." He started to sit up straight. Across from him, lying on the bed, was a way too thin blonde girl wearing Birkenstocks, a tie-dyed t-shirt and reeking of patchouli. Jackie had met her once before. Donna was her name. She was convinced Sean must be screwing Donna, since she knew they liked to drop acid together. That was a drug too far for Jackie. Right now they were across the room from each other, both sipping on Heinekens. It didn't smell like sex, so Jackie would have to be jealous without any real evidence to back it up.

"Hey guys. What's going on?" Jackie said this while falling into the beanbag, throwing her arms around Sean. Marking her territory. Donna seemed unimpressed.

"Donna was just telling me about this fascist professor she has."

Jackie grabbed Sean's beer and took a long sip. "How's that?"

"Well," Donna started, immediately angry, "it's my feminist literature class, which why is it taught by a fucking man anyway? But whatever, I figured we'd be reading *The Feminine Mystique* or Virginia Woolf or something by a woman. But this prick today wanted us to read passages from the Bible! The fucking Bible! And I said, what's feminist about this? He gave some crap about how it's some of the earliest pieces of literature we have and it's important to look at the way women were portrayed in it to understand future more progressive portrayals. And I'm like, religion is an oppressive, misogynist tool used to enslave us into thinking we should all be housewives or some shit. That I already know this from my own anecdotal experiences and don't want to be subjected to this fascist bullshit. He said, to fight for what's right in the future we must study the past. But I'm sick of the past. I'm sick of having my vagina owned. I'm not going to be further brainwashed by the Bible."

This was simultaneously the most adult-sounding thing Jackie had ever heard and also the stupidest.

"Fuck that guy," Jackie replied. This elicited a smile from Donna. She clearly liked the idea of a young feminist in her presence. Jackie looked at her beeper to check the time. "We've got to go if we're going to make the show?"

"Awe man, you don't still want to go to that. It's kid's stuff," Sean complained.

"The Scofflaws are the headliner, they're older than you."

"But I have to sit through some teenage ska band just to get to some older ska band. I don't even like ska."

"I don't like Phish and I let you play me their albums all the time."

"Are people going to be skanking?" he asked.

"It's a ska show. So, yes."

Sean was being a whiner, but that could only mean Jackie was winning. He had never complained like this. It was the kind of complaining you do when you know you have no choice but to do something you don't want to do.

"It's a big deal for my friend's band to be opening," Jackie continued. "I have to be there for them and I want you to come with me. And afterwards we have to stop by Sage's party. Half the senior class will be there."

81

Donna had a big grin on her face. She was loving this. Was it simply because a man was being told what to do, or did she just find it funny the guy they were both fucking couldn't talk his way out of it?

"I'm going to feel out of place. I'm so much older," he said.

"You're like two years older. You won't even be the oldest guy there," Jackie pointed out.

"High school kids have nothing to talk about."

"Maybe they don't understand philosophy like you guys do, but I have friends who know more about movies and music than you. And fuck you for calling them kids. It's demeaning. Am I a kid? Are you a kid fucker?"

Donna snorted with laughter. Sean's face dropped. Jackie knew he was already worried his peers thought this way about him. Now it was being discussed around the other woman he was probably sleeping with. The next time Donna was in bed with him, would she give him shit about it? Even if they weren't sleeping together there was no way a woman like Donna would let this go.

"You're either fucking a child," Jackie continued, "or you're dating a woman who wants you to take her to a show. Which is it?"

*****

"Why'd you have to put me on the spot in front of Donna like that?"

Sean was behind the wheel of his old VW, shockingly not a Beetle. The interior was littered with half-filled soda cans, candy wrappers and bags from Burger King and Taco Bell. Evidence of the late-night munchies. They were heading towards Huntington where that night, in the center of town, the streets would be closed off for a mini music festival. A who's who of the Long Island punk and ska scene, handpicked by Huntington's own The Scofflaws. This was the biggest show The Freaks had been booked on. Their star was rising.

"I shouldn't have to shame you to do things with me. And who cares what Donna thinks?" Jackie replied.

"She's cool. I, like, respect her."

Sean respected Donna, but did he respect Jackie? She cracked the window and lit a cigarette.

"Why are you embarrassed to go out with me?"

"Cause…people do look at you like you're a child." Jackie tried not to look offended. Sean continued. "You're not. *I* know that. But perception is reality, babe."

"I'm not asking for you to marry me. I'm just asking for you to be more considerate."

Sean thought for a moment and nodded. Was she finally getting through to him?

"Besides," she continued, "don't I get to show off that I'm not a kid anymore? That I date a real college man." Jackie ran her hand across his inner thigh. Sean, keeping his focus on the road, straightened up, reaching down to adjust his bulge. Right where Jackie wanted him.

"Fine. But don't expect me to like the music."

Music! Jackie had almost forgotten about her mixtape.

"I made you something." Jackie reached into her bag and pulled out a tape labeled "Sean's Rockin' Lady Mix." "Last night I put together a tape of all my favorite songs. And they're all female artists!"

Jackie watched Sean force a smile.

"Cool. I'll share it with Donna. She's always bitching about the patriarchy," he said.

Why was he bringing up Donna? And what did the patriarchy have to do with this? The songs were emotional regardless of gender. You just had to be human. Jackie popped in the tape.

"Do you like Tori Amos?"

"Cornflake Girl" came through the speakers. Sean grimaced. This was *not* a good solution.

"What's wrong?" Jackie asked.

"I could never get into her."

"Did you ever *really* listen though?"

"What's the big deal? You don't like my music," Sean said.

"I mean *really* gave it a listen. Are you listening? Her voice is a combination of extreme strength and extreme vulnerability. Who else sounds like this?"

"I don't get it," Sean said sourly.

This is not really happening.

Jackie was not going to be discouraged. Maybe Tori wasn't for everyone. She decided to fast-forward a bit before hitting play again. "Fuck and Run." Quickly she stopped it and kept fast-forwarding. Right now her heart wouldn't be able to take his college dissection of her favorite song. She pressed play. L7. *"Shitlist."*

Anyone with a pulse would rock out to this song. Apparently Sean was dead. He reached over and lowered the volume.

"It's too loud, babe. And too angry. Who wants that much rage ruining a mellow vibe?"

"Sometimes you need to rage. Don't you ever get angry?" she asked.

"Sure. But I don't want to wallow in it. These chicks are wallowing in it. They have an agenda. They scream and yell and want to unsettle you. Then you get angry and need to buy their records because they've tricked you into thinking they speak for your anger, when they're the ones who got you so angry in the first place! Fuck, see, I'm getting angry just listening to it."

Sean leaned over and turned off the stereo.

"That doesn't make any sense," Jackie said.

"It does. Believe me. I'm taking a marketing course," Sean responded confidently.

"No. I get what you're saying but you can make that claim about anything. Phish puts you in a mellow mood so you keep buying their records because they've tricked you into thinking they speak for your mellow-*ness*. Or whatever."

"But who wants to be hateful?" Sean said.

"Hate and anger are different things," Jackie countered. "I'm angry at you for not giving my mix a fair chance, but I don't hate you for it."

"Look, I just don't dig female singers." What the fuck was Sean talking about? Not to worry, he tried to explain. "I know I'm like this really progressive guy. But there are certain taste things you can't explain. Just like how you don't like jam bands, I don't like hearing women sing."

"Janice Joplin?"

"She's alright, I guess."

"Madonna?"

"Pop garbage."

Jackie felt exasperated. How had this never come up? Maybe she was the one who should be embarrassed to be out with him.

"I understand not liking a genre of music," she relented, "but this tape has all types of music."

"Chick singers *are* a type of music. They're all just kind of pop. I took a history of twentieth century music course, so I was exposed to like, a lot of different singers. And all the women sounded the same to me."

"That's incredibly sexist."

"How?"

Jackie knew it was sexist, but couldn't explain it. She had yet to take a course in debating douchebags. She needed a counterexample.

"It's like saying, all black women look alike. So if you're not into one black woman you'd be into none of them? That'd be racist." Jackie was fairly certain this argument didn't quite work, but she went with it anyway.

"Well...I dated a black chick—"

"Congrats, you're so fucking cool." Jackie's voice dripped with sarcasm.

"And I wouldn't do it again."

"What?!? Why not?"

"I found out I'm not attracted to black women," Sean said, far too matter-of-factly.

Jackie's head was about to explode. "So if Naomi Campbell wanted to sleep with you, you wouldn't do it?"

"Not attracted to her."

"You're insane."

"I have an aversion to black vaginas. They're different looking."

"Yeah, because they're not white. Not because they're ugly."

"You ever date a black guy?'

"No. But not because I'm not attracted to them. It's just because I don't know any. What kind of laidback racist progressive are you?"

"If I'm more attracted to brunettes than blondes, am I a racist against blondes? No. It's the same thing."

"NO IT'S NOT!"

"How is it different? I prefer eating white pussy as opposed to black pussy because it's more aesthetically pleasing to me. But I'd never tell anyone else they were wrong to prefer black pussy."

"This conversation is making me very uncomfortable. I know you're wrong. I just can't explain why."

"Maybe one day you'll get what I'm saying."

Stupidly, Jackie had forgotten she was just a dumb kid.

Jeff

Mallrats.

Friday was the worst day to work at the video store because of mallrats. That was the day they came out in droves, starting their weekend of being loiterers. And Movieland was located next to the food court, which made it mallrat central.

The mallrats were mostly delinquent kids with nowhere else to go on a Friday night other than wander the mall causing trouble. They'd try and steal things from the stores, trash the food court and generally be obnoxious and unpleasant. Jeff knew some of them from school, but since the Smith Haven Mall was the nicest mall for miles around, mallrats attending schools all over the area flocked here. Smith Haven had just redone its food court, adding a Taco Bell, and there's nothing mallrats love more than cheap tacos. It was also the first mall in the area to have a Hot Topic, and featured the largest Spencer Gifts on Long Island. The high volume of sexually explicit gag gifts made Spencer's the favorite store of immature mallrats. Who didn't want to buy gummy candies shaped like penises?

Vic was the assistant manager at Movieland. Being second rung on this admittedly short corporate ladder meant he was often stuck working the late afternoon/evening shift on Fridays. And since Vic knew Jeff wouldn't squeal on him for his overall laziness, he'd often schedule Jeff for Fridays as well. More than once Jeff walked into work finding Vic asleep behind the counter. He'd wake him by shouting, "The district manager is here!" It would get Vic every time. To make the shifts go faster, they'd often play a game called "What's down Vic's pants?" in which Vic would take a tape off the shelf, shove it down the front of his pants, and make Jeff play twenty questions to figure out the title.

Today Jeff was working a short shift. He'd put in to get off by seven in order to make it to The Freaks show on time. Good. With the events of the day Jeff knew the mallrats would be lashing out, unsure what to do with themselves. It was barely four o'clock and they were already all over the store, pissing off Vic. As Jeff entered, tucking his white Movieland polo into his standard uniform black pants, Vic was already fighting with a mallrat.

"What's the deal with this movie?" A kid, no more than fourteen, dressed in baggy pants and a knit cap with a pot leaf on it, was waving a copy of *Pretty in Pink* in Vic's face.

"What do ya mean?" Vic said in his usual gruff tone, already annoyed he was being asked a question.

"Is it a gay movie?" The mallrat was snickering. Whatever the joke was, at least he thought it was funny.

"What?"

"Is it a movie for gay people? Like do faggots watch this?"

Vic grabbed the tape violently from his hand and pointed to the exit.

"Get the fuck outta my store!" Vic demanded.

"Why? I was just asking a question. Is it a movie for faggots?"

"I SAID GET OUT! FUCK OFF! YOU'RE BANNED FOR LIFE!"

This was typical of Vic. He made a game of screaming at kids and banning them for life, seeing how many he could kick out of the store in one shift. Luckily none of them ever complained to the higher ups. Even if they did, Vic would just deny it. Jeff loved watching this. It was everything he wanted to do to these little jerks but couldn't.

"Your store sucks anyway. I'm going to Blockbuster." The kid marched out, eyeballing Jeff as he left.

"Good! The people at Blockbuster are just as fucking stupid as you!" Vic then noticed Jeff. "Oh, hey Jeff. How goes it?" Just like that Vic could turn it off. His whole attitude was an act. Working a low-paying job at Movieland was his version of performance art.

"What was that about?" Jeff asked.

"Fucking kids."

Jeff headed behind the counter and started to count his register.

"So listen," Vic continued. "I'm supposed to give you the whole speech about how management wants you to consider coming on full time this summer as an assistant manager."

Jeff sighed. "We've been over this. I'm not spending my last summer before college working here forty hours a week. I don't want that level of responsibility."

"Responsibility? Have you *seen* me work?" Vic said.

"I just don't want to be stuck managing a video store in the mall. It's pathetic."

"Thanks a lot."

"I didn't mean...you know what I mean," Jeff said.

"I don't blame you. But like I said, management wanted me to ask, so I asked."

For three months Jeff had been asked at least once a week if he'd be willing to take on more responsibility. He was already so much more responsible than everyone else he knew. If he was going to be responsible about anything more it'd either be making a movie or falling in love. Manager at a mall video store didn't fit into his plan.

*****

It was getting close to Jeff's break. Soon Katie would be stopping by and they'd grab a bite to eat. Until that time, Jeff was struggling to maintain his sanity dealing with the public. He hated customers who knew nothing about the films they were looking for. The most popular question lately was, "What's that one about the Holocaust? Do you have that?" How do you not know *Schindler's List*? Do you keep your head in the sand? It's still in theaters, for crying out loud. However, right now he was dealing with a woman who had no idea what movie to get for her children.

"How old are your kids?" Jeff politely asked.

"Six and four," she replied.

"Hmmm." Jeff's eyes scanned the children's section. "Do they like The Muppets?"

"I don't know?" How did this woman not know if her children liked The Muppets? The only way her kids would have even seen The Muppets was if she had shown them.

"I used to love The Muppets," Jeff said. "I still do. Everyone does. Why don't you start them off with the original *Muppet*

Movie?" Jeff handed her the tape, adorned with images of Kermit, Miss Piggy and of course his favorite, Gonzo.

"I don't know this one," the woman said quizzically.

You've got to be kidding me.

"Sure you do. It's the story of how The Muppets met. They go to Hollywood." The mother stared at Jeff like he was insane. "'The Rainbow Connection'"?

"What's that?" she asked.

Jeff was getting annoyed, but you'd never know it by his chipper demeanor.

"The song Kermit sings." She still looked lost. Jeff didn't know how else to explain it other than to actually sing it. Would he really subject this woman to his awful singing voice? Screw it. It was her own fault for not knowing The Muppets. She was asking for it.

It was off key but Jeff began warbling his way through. He sang about lovers. He sang about dreamers. He sang about himself. It was the first time as a teenager he'd actually said the lyrics out loud, and the emotions behind them hit him in a way they never had before.

Upon finishing, applause echoed through the store. Jeff peered behind the clueless mother to see Katie standing in the entrance, clapping wildly.

*****

They sat across from each other in the center of the busy food court, Jeff eating his softshell tacos and Katie her bean burrito. She was a vegetarian and Taco Bell was the number-one fast food option of vegetarians too.

"Let's say," Katie started, "you met a girl. And she is the hottest girl you've ever seen."

"Go on."

"And she's super smart too. Basically she's everything you ever wanted in a girl. But she has trimethylaminuria."

"What's that?" Jeff asked.

"It's a disease where you constantly smell like fish."

"That's a real thing? You just go around your whole life smelling like fish."

"Yes. It's horrible and it's gross. Everything about this girl is perfect except she constantly smells awful. Would you date her?"

Jeff didn't hesitate. "Sure."

"Really? She smells like fish *constantly*," Katie said with surprise.

"No one's perfect. If she's so great in every other way, I'd probably get used to the smell, right?"

Katie decided to raise the stakes.

"What if she smelled like shit? Like actual human feces."

"Again, I'd probably get used to the smell."

"You're disgusting."

The two of them chuckled a bit. These ridiculous hypotheticals had become Jeff's favorite part of hanging out with Katie. They showcased her humor and creativity. Now however, it was time for Jeff to do a little fishing of his own.

"Where'd you come up with this one? Did someone with trim...thy...lam..."

"Trimethylaminuria."

"Did someone with that horrible ailment ask you out or something?" he asked.

It was a pretty blatant way to see where her head was at in terms of dating. It was also a risk. Jeff wanted to seem concerned about the future of her love life, but not *too* concerned. Talking to girls was like walking a tightrope.

"Worse," she said. "Harold Berlangieri asked me out."

"Big Berl asked you out?" The whole Long Island music scene knew Big Berl. He'd gotten this nickname not because he was fat or larger than life. He got it because he was so damn old. Harold "Big Berl" Berlangieri had just turned twenty-five. And yet he spent most of his time hanging around all-ages punk shows. It was weird. Jeff and Katie had attended his most recent birthday party. It was at his parents' house and at least half the guests were still in high school. At one point in the night Katie turned to Jeff and asked, "What the fuck are we doing here?" Jeff agreed. Big Berl was ancient. To still be living at home at twenty-five and hanging out with seventeen-year-olds was pathetic. At the very least it was a cautionary tale.

"Right? He's so old. And creepy," Katie said.

"Is it even legal?" Jeff asked.

"That's how he started his essay! It said, 'I'm well aware the eight-year age difference between us may be an obstacle for me to overcome, but the age of consent in New York State is seventeen years old.'"

"He asked you out in an essay?"

"Yes!" Katie exclaimed. "It was five pages long. But it gave me a good idea. All these guys are starting to ask me out."

"Really?" This was what Jeff feared the most. Maybe Nick was wrong. Maybe he had to beat these other guys to the punch. No. Nick knew best. Patience.

"Yeah," Katie continued. "I didn't realize how in demand I was. Anyway, I have to narrow down my suitors. So I've decided to have an essay competition! A thousand words on why I should date you."

She said this with such pride and excitement. Like it was the best way anyone had ever come up with to choose a potential mate. Jeff was not as enthusiastic.

"Wait, so whoever writes the best essay gets to…date you?" he questioned.

"Yup!"

Jeff was a terrific writer. He knew it. He also had genuine feelings for Katie that he could channel into a great essay. But he didn't want to be in competition for her heart. He wanted her to simply want him, like he wanted her. Jeff couldn't hide his contempt for this experiment.

"That's really dumb. It's a dumb idea."

Katie looked hurt. "I thought you'd think it was fun. I was going to ask you to help me grade the essays."

Friend zoned.

"The person who wants you, you should know in your heart how they feel. And how you feel about them. There'd be no reason to put it in an essay because their actions would speak louder than words."

Katie looked Jeff dead in the eyes. "The person who is unwilling to write me an essay would lose a lot of points right off the bat."

Was Katie asking Jeff to write an essay? Of course not. She just asked him to help judge the essay competition. Don't take the bait. Wait her out.

"Are people really going to write essays about why you should date them?" Jeff questioned.

Katie motioned to a table on the other side of the food court. One of the Hodrinskys was furiously writing.

"He came into the store to ask me out and I told him to write an essay about why I should date him. Now he is. *That's* love."

"That's not love. That's stupidity." Jeff was starting to get flustered. Keep it together. "You don't even know which one that is. Do you *really* want to go out with a Hodrinsky?"

"Maybe," Katie coyly replied.

"No. No you don't."

"Jeff, you don't know what I want."

He didn't and he shouldn't push the issue any further.

"I'm just saying," he continued, "I wouldn't want to be forced to write an essay to win a girl's heart. She's either interested or not."

"No one's asking you to write an essay. Unless you wanted to."

Wait a second, was Katie implying she wanted Jeff to throw his hat into the ring? Ask her out. Just do it right now.

"That's alright," he said.

Stick with the plan. Let her get all these essays out of her system. They'll all be idiotic and Jeff would be there to point that out. Then he'd be the last man standing.

Katie got up to head back to work.

"Oh, I almost forgot." She threw a button down onto the table. It landed with a metallic clang. "I made this for you. I know you were a big fan. Sorry about Kurt."

It was another button. The cover to the album *Nevermind*. Instead of "Smells Like Teen Spirit" Katie had written "Smells Like Teen Farts." To complete the picture she added stink lines coming from the naked baby's butt. Jeff immediately attached it to his polo shirt, just below the Movieland logo.

*****

The last hour of a shift at a dead-end job is always the longest. A lot of clock-watching no matter how busy things are. Jeff only had twenty minutes left, then he'd head over to The Freaks show. He was going back and forth questioning if he had made the right call in regard to Katie. They were both working tomorrow night. He'd feel her out then.

Vic had left him alone to run the store while he went outside to have a cigarette. Of course that's when things finally started getting busy. Jeff was checking customers out in a robotic way. Next. Your total will be eight seventy-two. Next. Your total will be four twenty-seven. At times like this Jeff couldn't watch the floor, and he was convinced some mallrat was probably shoplifting. Finally Vic returned and immediately jumped on the other register, checking out customers with even less enthusiasm than Jeff.

"Shit. Sorry man. Didn't think we'd suddenly get slammed."

"It's alright. Pretty soon you'll have to deal with this all by yourself," Jeff reminded him.

"Fuck, that's right. You're out of here in what? Twenty? I'm locking up alone? Fucking bullshit, man."

The customers in line didn't seem to care for the language being used but would never dare say so. Not with Vic just itching to yell at them.

"So," Vic continued, "that Katie chick from Hot Topic, is she single now?"

"Why? She ask you to write an essay?"

"What? No. What the fuck you talking about?" Vic said.

"Nothing," Jeff said. "Why do you ask?"

"I just saw her making out with some guy in the parking lot."

If time was moving slowly before, it now came to a complete stop.

"What?" Jeff asked, stunned.

"Yeah. I thought she was dating that Dennis douchebag but I just saw her with that friend of yours."

"A friend of mine?!?"

"Yeah. That weirdo who comes in here. In a band. Wears a dirty blazer and smells like shit."

No, no, no, no, no, no, no, no, no. That can't be right. Nick should be with the band right now. And why would he be making out with Katie? Nick could literally have any woman he wanted. Why would he pick the girl he knew Jeff liked? Vic had to be wrong.

Jeff turned away from the customers and grabbed Vic by the collar, studying his face.

"Are you sure it was Nick?"

"Unless you've got other friends who wear shitty blazers and smell like shit," Vic replied.

Trimethylaminuria. Jeff didn't say another word. Instead he abandoned his post, racing around the counter and running out of the store, leaving Vic alone to deal with a long line of confused customers.

"Where the fuck are you going?" Vic yelled.

At full speed Jeff raced into Hot Topic. He slammed his hands down on the counter, startling the Goth employee and interrupting a customer asking a question about spiked dog collars.

"Where's Katie?" Jeff said, panic in his voice.

"She left for the day."

Jeff could have screamed, but instead thanked the Goth and headed back to Movieland. Nick had just ruined Jeff's plan. His whole timetable would have to be thrown away. He had no choice but to tell Katie how he felt. Tonight. Immediately. She needed to know what Nick had done. That he was a scumbag who would undermine a friend without a second thought. Was Nick even a friend? Had he ever been?

"What are you fucking doing?" Vic shouted again as Jeff ran into the store's back office, slamming the door in anger.

He pulled out his wallet and removed a tiny piece of paper. It was folded up and covered in nearly microscopic handwriting. A list of all his friends' phone numbers. He looked for Katie's. Should he really be calling her? Yes. He had to find out if it was true. Would she even be home yet?

He dialed the number. The answering machine.

"You've reached the Katie Keating fan club!

Please leave a message."

Katie had her own line so anything he said would only be heard by her, but did he really want to leave a message? Jeff hung up. Rage overwhelmed him. Clearly he wasn't thinking straight. He dialed again.

"You've reached the Katie Keating fan club!

Please leave a message."

"Hey Katie, it's Jeff...Rosenduft. Anyway, sorry for giving you a hard time earlier. You left before I could ask you if you wanted to go to The Freaks show tonight. Or maybe you're already going.

Maybe you're going with Nick. Vic said he saw you two in the parking lot, *soooo*, I don't know. There's something you should know about Nick. And about me too, I guess. We need to talk."

T.J.

The town of Smithtown, Long Island had a population of 113,406, ninety-five percent of which was white. In fact, it would be hard to think of a single black student who went to Smithtown High School. T.J. often wondered if that made the town indirectly racist. There were plenty of Asians though.

Smithtown was founded in 1665 by Richard Smith. Legend has it he rescued an Indian princess (every story about Long Island seemed to involve an Indian princess), and as a reward her father, the chief, would give Richard Smith all the land he could cover while riding from sunrise to sunset on a bull. Smith, being the clever white man he was, chose the summer solstice as his day. The land became known as Smithtown. To commemorate this event there is a large statue of a bull in the center of town. You can tell it's a bull because it is *extremely* anatomically correct. The bull's name is Whisper.

T.J. had lived in Smithtown his entire life. So had most of the people he knew. He and Jeff went all the way back to the first grade at Dogwood Elementary School. They used to play games like TV Tag at recess and would ride their bikes into town every day, scrounging up enough change for Italian ice.

The Smithtown school district had three middle schools and two high schools. High School East and High School West. Despite being in the same town, the two schools were fierce rivals. As children T.J. and Jeff only had to deal with this rivalry on Halloween. Every Halloween they lived in fear that while out trick or treating, somehow they'd get caught in the crossfire of an East/West fight. There was a rumor that before they were born, teenagers from Smithtown West killed an East kid in the woods behind Dogwood Elementary by forcing him to swallow rocks. To be on the safe side T.J. and Jeff always armed themselves with shaving cream and eggs. Thank God they never had to use them.

They began to drift apart in middle school. Early in the two best friends' time at Nesaquake Middle School, the district did a funny thing. They decided to combine the two high schools into one. There would be peace at last. This also meant they would combine all three middle schools into what would become the largest middle school in the country.

With triple the normal number of students, T.J. and Jeff weren't scheduled in the same classes. They didn't even have the same lunch period. Middle school turned out to be the loneliest time of T.J.'s life. He struggled to make new friends. This caused him to disengage from all academic activity. He floated by as a D student. One day at lunch, his table was talking about "douching." Nobody really knew what the word meant, it was just a funny word that seemed dirty. On a dare, T.J., in front of his entire table, asked stuck-up Miss Catalanotto, "Do you douche?" The question got a roar of laughter and T.J. three days of detention. It would have been more, but all involved were fairly certain T.J. had no idea what he was even asking.

And thus T.J. found his calling. He was the kid who accepted any dare. From the trivial, sticking ten Warheads in his mouth at once, to the more extreme, streaking a girls' field hockey game. This new lifestyle did not improve his academic record.

Once high school came around T.J. had a solid, delinquent group of friends. They spent most of their day cutting class and hanging out in the school's video room. In an age when the arts were starting to lose funding, Smithtown had a terrific film and video department. A huge room, tucked away at the back of the school. It had televisions, all the movies you could watch, VHS camcorders, video editing equipment and big comfy sofas to sit on. It even had its own air conditioning unit because video equipment needed to be kept cool. The film teacher, Mrs. Benson, had a don't ask, don't tell policy. She never asked if you were cutting class, and if you didn't tell she'd let you hang out there all day long. T.J. signed up for some classes and spent the next four years hiding out in the video room. This is where he reunited with Jeff.

Jeff actually took the film classes to learn. Even back at Dogwood, Jeff was always writing stories. Once he discovered filmmaking, it became his storytelling vehicle of choice. It seemed certain Jeff was going to make it.

Quickly the two old friends fell back into the same old relationship. It was like the last three years had never happened. Jeff hadn't changed a bit. He dressed the same, even had the same haircut he did in fifth grade. He was a solid student who was focused on his dreams. T.J. was shocked that Jeff wanted to hang with him. That he wanted to go to punk shows in Seth's garage and spend time with stoned assholes who thought it was funny to fart on each other. It felt like some unnecessary Dogwood loyalty. After four years though, it just seemed like Jeff enjoyed people in a shockingly non-judgmental way.

In September Jeff was going to move to the city and start going to film school. T.J. knew he'd still see him occasionally but it was about to be middle school all over again. What made it worse was T.J. wasn't going anywhere. He wasn't even going to Suffolk Community College. He just was going to exist in a perpetual state of un-ambition. Maybe he'd move to the city too? Get a job at a Blockbuster or Tower Records. Maybe even star in some of Jeff's films.

Jeff was a huge Nirvana fan. Like really huge. Like has a giant poster of Kurt Cobain pointing a gun, hanging over his bed huge.

Like had been the only person T.J. knew who actually saw them in concert huge. Why hadn't T.J. mentioned Kurt to him back at Seth's?

Fuck. Jeff must be pretty sad today.

*****

Liz sampled every flavor of Slurpee before settling on cherry. T.J. chose Coke. There was an unspoken decision between them to wander the 7-11 and refill the icy beverages before they left. The apathetic clerk wouldn't care.

They strolled past a selection of Campbell's soup. Was it too late to ask what soup scalded young Liz?

"So...if you don't like going to shows, what do you do for fun?" This question from T.J. seemed far less intrusive.

"I like going to shows. Just not tonight. Tonight I want to let loose!" She jumped a little as she said this. Her manic energy was intoxicating.

"When you're not letting loose though, what do you do?" he asked.

"I don't know what you mean."

"What? I mean, what do you do?" T.J. asked again.

"Huh?"

Did Liz honestly not understand the question or was she just fucking with him?

"Like, we go hang out at the mall sometimes. Or we go to diners. See shows or movies. Mini golf," T.J explained.

"Mini golf?"

T.J. was being judged. Can't punk/Goth/stoner kids enjoy mini golf? He had no idea what to do with this girl, and he hoped a suggestion would spark an interest in her.

"On Fridays we sometimes go to Rock N Bowl," he said.

"What's that? And who's the 'we' you keep mentioning?" Liz asked.

"I hang with a pretty big crew." T.J. said. "Most of them are going to the show and then this party at our friend Sage's place tonight. She's got this huge house in Nissequogue and—"

"I don't have a crew. I mean I did but I don't hang with them anymore."

This must have had something to do with drugs or suicide, but again T.J decided not to press.

"Maybe our crew can be your new crew?" he suggested.

"What's Rock N Bowl?" she asked again.

"It's just bowling, but they play music and turn on strobe lights and shit. It's kinda swiss."

"I could do that," Liz agreed.

Apparently miniature golf was below her but bowling was not.

"Hey!" Liz exclaimed. "We should throw more Sunny Doodles at people!"

She gestured towards a selection of Drake's products. T.J. wasn't going to say no to this or any other suggestion she made. As frustrating as this conversation had been, the idea of pleasing this girl was all he cared about. Keep the evening going. On a long enough timeline he'd get an opportunity to make out with her.

"No," T.J. said while studying the cakes. "I have a better idea."

He reached for a box of Yodels. These were always his favorite. A cylinder-shaped chocolate cake, filled with vanilla cream, covered in a hard chocolate shell. T.J.'s mom used to pack them in his lunch every day growing up. Always delicious but even better frozen. You could keep your Devil Dogs and Ring Dings, Yodels were the best, and the best for what T.J. had in mind.

T.J. paid and the two of them headed outside. As he started the car, the mixtape fired back up. It was a complete 180 in tone from KMFDM. "Disarm" by The Smashing Pumpkins. T.J. loved the melancholic state the whole *Siamese Dream* album put him in. But this was no time for infinite sadness. This was time to let loose.

He ripped a Yodel out of its plastic packaging and leaned out the window.

"Yodelayheehoo!"

T.J. fired a Yodel at the front door of 7-11. It exploded in a mess of vanilla cream and chocolate frosting. Liz shrieked with delight. He threw the car in drive, peeling out of the parking lot and down Main Street before the store clerk even realized where the mess he'd have to clean up came from. T.J. went to this 7-11 almost every morning for his breakfast Slurpee so there might have been a twinge of remorse. What's remorse for a small mess compared to the joy he had just given a lonely girl.

"My turn." Liz removed a Yodel from its packaging and rolled down her window.

"You have to yell yodelayheehoo before you throw it," T.J. reminded her.

Up ahead was a middle-aged woman exiting a low-end department store. T.J slowed down.

"Yodelayheehoo!"

The unusual call caused the woman to look up. Liz fired the Yodel but came up short. It pathetically landed at the woman's feet as the car slowly rolled by.

"You have to stop the car," Liz complained.

On the corner stood an older man, with a beer belly, wearing a mechanic's uniform. This time T.J. stopped the car right in front of him.

"Yodelayheehoo!"

The target was so close Liz couldn't miss. She nailed him right in his fat belly. The man was too confused and upset to even get out a "fuck you" before the two Yodelers drove off.

Liz grabbed T.J.'s arm, shaking it, thrilled with what she had just done. If Liz would grab him with such excitement every time she threw a Yodel, T.J. would give her a billion Yodels to throw.

"Did you see his fucking face? Did you?" she screamed.

"The fat fuck is probably gonna eat it," he responded.

T.J. was being cruel. For all his usual who-gives-a-fuck bluster, he didn't think of himself as a cruel person. Sure, he'd pants someone on a dare and apparently kicked a guy in the back of the head once, but he wouldn't talk shit behind people's backs. Fat fuck? This wasn't him.

It'd been nineteen months and thirteen days since T.J. last had sex. Since then there'd mostly been awkward, drunken make-out sessions at shows or parties. There'd been even more awkward attempts at hitting on girls. T.J. often came on too strong and would scare girls away with his blunt insanity. Hell, he was the kind of guy who would throw himself off a roof to get your attention. They smelled it on him, how desperate he was to just be near them.

Last summer he had come on to Jackie Spampinato and said some things he regretted. Jackie had a bit of an unfair reputation for being easy. One night at the diner, in front of half a dozen friends, Jackie realized she'd forgotten her money and couldn't pay for her Belgian waffle. T.J. offered to pay in exchange for a blowjob. Jackie gave him the coldest of stares and didn't say a word for the rest of the night to anyone. She was so mad because she knew it wasn't just a bad joke. She knew there was truth to it. That deep down T.J. thought there was a chance she'd actually give him a blowjob for a Belgian waffle. And that if she had said yes, T.J. would have let her do it because he was that desperate to get off. Was this really what he thought of her? He never apologized and neither one ever mentioned it again, but Jackie never greeted him as warmly as she used to. Maybe T.J. was crueler than he thought?

"Yodelayheehoo!" Liz sent a Yodel soaring through the air. Splat! A direct hit to Whisper the bull. She was really getting the hang of this.

T.J. turned to Liz. The sun was finally setting behind her. She smiled a slightly off-kilter smile. The image was beautiful.

"So are you taking me to the Rock N Bowl or what?"

Jeff

Betrayal.

Nick had his flaws, but Jeff never realized just how big a piece of human garbage he was. That he'd backstab a friend just to kiss a girl he probably didn't even want. Or did he? Would Katie be the rare girl for him that he wouldn't treat like a one-night stand? The rare girl he'd actually date for a while?

Speeding down the road in his Taurus, Jeff was breaking every traffic law to get to the show before it started. If Katie wasn't there at least he could confront Nick. Would this jerk even have the balls to admit what he'd done? Jeff wanted to call him out in front of the whole band. They'd see Nick for what he was. It would rattle him and they'd have a terrible show. Nick would be blamed for ruining an important gig and kicked out of The Freaks. Jeff didn't expect that actually to happen, did he? It was just a beautiful fantasy.

Wait a minute, what the hell was Jeff doing? Katie was her own person. She could make out with whoever she wanted. And what was with that message he'd left? What would Katie hearing that accomplish? Would hearing a nervous, desperate teenage boy whine about how his friend backstabbed him suddenly make Jeff desirable?

Maybe?

At this point Jeff had to keep going forward. He had to explain to Katie how much of a scumbag Nick was and then ask her out himself. It was an awkward, messy plan. Far more awkward than if he had just confessed his feelings early, like an adult. Jeff often speculated how one day this would be so much easier. Older people aren't crippled by insecurities like teenagers are. They can just walk up to a woman and ask her out. And if television had taught us anything, adult women would be more likely to say yes. Hell, even George Costanza got laid regularly. Sure…this was how things worked.

But it didn't matter. Hopefully Jeff wouldn't have to worry about dating in his adult future. Hopefully Katie was *the one*.

The streets were packed and there was no place to park near the center of town, so Jeff had a good ten-minute walk ahead of him to get to the stage. The Freaks were supposed to go on in eight minutes, but no show in the history of shows has ever started on time. Jeff ran down the street, dodging pedestrians. It was only then that he realized he was still wearing his uniform. Still wearing his "Smells Like Teen Farts" button. He had raced out of work before his shift had even ended. Luckily Vic had no work ethic, he'd understand.

No one on stage yet. Good. They must be behind it. Jeff headed towards a cheap white curtain that protected the bands from their adoring public. He tried to race through the curtain, getting tangled up in it. Arms flailing, he attempted to free himself from the twisted fabric. His eyes were blinded by a sea of white. Finally, he spun around, awkwardly unwrapping himself. There in front of him stood his friends The Freaks. Donnie, Donnie's younger brother Bobby, Chris, Sean, and his enemy Nick LeWinter. Nick spotted Jeff immediately. His eyes widened and the cigarette dangling from his lips nearly dropped. Nick knew he deserved what was coming.

The Freaks seemed like they were in the middle of a pre-show meeting that Jeff was more than willing to disrupt. Love trumps all.

"What the hell, Nick?" Jeff said as the whole band stared at him. Nick said nothing, so Jeff continued. "You didn't think I'd find out? What's wrong with you?"

"Fuck you, Nick," Bobby the drummer said. "What bullshit did you pull now?"

"Nothing," Nick said. "I mean, nothing that bad."

"You want to know what your buddy Nick did?" Jeff asked angrily.

"Let me guess," Chris said. "It's about Katie Keating."

Jeff was about to explode. How did he already know about this? Luckily, Chris would explain. "He was late getting here and he told me it was because he was busy feeling up Katie in the mall parking lot."

Nick had nothing to say. He just stood there, staring at his shoes with a dumb look on his face.

"Did he tell you the part about how I came to him only a few hours ago asking his advice on when to ask her out? Did he tell you that?"

"Yeah," Chris said. "Actually he did. He said he felt kinda guilty about it."

"WHAT?!?" Jeff got right in Nick's face. Nick still refused to make eye contact. "You felt guilty about it? You had enough sense to know it was wrong but you still did it. Why? Why did you do it?"

Nick just shrugged his shoulders. This caused Jeff to throw his arms in the air and scream in frustration.

"You're a really crappy friend, you know that. You're just, just a horrible, horrible person. Everyone knows it. Jackie. T.J. Your bandmates. They always tell me not to trust you. That you're not a real friend. But I didn't want to listen. Because I'm an idiot."

Nick still wasn't reacting. Jeff had just told him everyone he knew thought he was trash and Nick didn't even flinch.

"So," Jeff continued, "how long after I told you I was in love with Katie did you decide to hook up with her? I mean, you had to move pretty quickly."

"Well, I did," Nick finally responded. "I knew what time she got off work so figured I'd meet her then. I also knew I'd be cutting it close with the show, but I always wanted to make out with her. If you guys started dating I might never get the chance. So I calculated that it was worth the risk."

"Worth the risk to our friendship?" Jeff was exasperated.

"I didn't anticipate you'd find out so soon. I figured you'd either discover it once you two were dating or once she rejected you. Either way, at that point I figured you'd be too happy or too sad to care."

"And how did you, in that minuscule window, get her to make out with you?" Jeff asked, sounding more curious than upset to hear the answer.

"I said, 'I hear you're single, do you want to make out' and she said 'sure.'"

The simplicity of what Nick had done infuriated Jeff. So did the honesty and callousness with which he spoke.

"Is she here?" Jeff asked.

"No."

"Are you planning on fooling around with her again?"

"Maybe."

"You know, now I have to confess my love to her. I have no choice but to move up my timetable."

"Jeff," Donnie interrupted. "I'm sorry about all this but we've got a show to play and you wandered into the middle of a group…disagreement."

There was no grand denouncement of Nick's actions. No kicking him out of the band. No one even coming to Jeff's aid. It was suddenly business as usual for the band. As if Jeff never interrupted.

"Look," Chris said, "it's the only thing on any music lover's mind. We have to address it."

"Fine," Donnie offered, "address it. Go out there and say something like, 'We love you Kurt' or 'This one's for Kurt,' but we're not covering a Nirvana song."

Oh, that's right, Kurt Cobain was dead. So much had been happening it was easy to forget.

"Why not? The crowd would eat it up," Chris argued.

"Why not? Because we don't know how to play any fucking Nirvana songs. We're not a goddamn grunge band!" Donnie's frustrations with his bandmate were clear.

"I'm just saying, we can put our own punk or ska twist on 'Teen Spirit.' You *know* the other bands are thinking of doing something. We go on first, let's be the trendsetters," Chris argued.

"I get it. You don't want to be the odd band out but I guarantee the other bands aren't going to play any Nirvana covers because I guarantee they don't know any either. If you feel this strongly about it, we can learn 'Lithium' or 'About a Girl' and play it at the next show. People will still be upset that he's dead a week from now," Donnie said.

"Wait a minute," Bobby joined in. "I'm a fucking musician. I can figure out how to jam out a version of a Nirvana song. We all can. We've heard the songs a million times."

Donnie did not look happy that his brother wasn't backing him up.

"Thank you," Chris said, feeling validated.

"But there's the booker for that battle of the bands out there," Sean said. "We don't want to mess up in front of him."

"All the more reason to pay tribute to the most popular band of our generation," Chris rebutted. *"The crowd would eat it up."*

A few of the band members had glanced over to see Jeff eavesdropping. They didn't seem to care. Jeff seemed desperate to join in the discussion, but first he wanted to hear what Nick had to say. Whatever that was, Jeff would push the opposite and try to turn this disagreement into an outright fight. Why? Same reason Nick made out with Katie. Because he could.

"What about you, Nick?" Jeff asked. "What say you?"

Nick looked at the faces of his bandmates. He sighed. "I don't think it's a good idea. Let's just stick with the set list."

Before Chris could open his mouth, Jeff fired back.

"You're supposed to be this big musical genius. Most talented guy in the band. You always say that, don't you?" Nick looked down at the ground, sheepishly. Jeff continued. "But here you are not up for the simple challenge of playing a Nirvana song? Give me a break. It's pathetic."

Jeff knew he wasn't being subtle, obviously trying to create band jealousy. He also was certain it wouldn't work. The Freaks already knew Nick thought he was better than the rest of them. The Freaks also knew he was right.

"I would prefer not to." Nick spoke quietly, unsure how to handle this.

"Come on. Give the people what they want," Jeff said.

"There's no keyboard part. What will I play?" Nick asked.

"Improvise."

Nick looked at his bandmates for help. Jeff was now calling the shots for The Freaks. No one seemed to mind.

"What song?" Nick finally relented. "Not 'Teen Spirit.'"

"'Rape Me,'" Jeff suggested. "It's short and it's simple but also instantly recognizable."

The Freaks started to look at each other, slowly nodding their heads with approval.

"Do you know the words?" Nick asked Chris in an accusatory tone.

"Of course I do!" Chris said this as if it was the stupidest question he'd ever been asked. "*Rape me...bah bah bah bah bah*

*bah...yada yada....*yeah, I know it. And what I don't know, I'll just kind of mumble, like Kurt."

This response did not instill confidence in Chris' bandmates. Nick looked like he was about to object again when Jeff cut him off with words of "encouragement."

"You guys will be great. Get out there and rape this audience!"

Chris, full of adrenaline, bounded up onto the stage. Donnie, Bobby and Sean followed. Nick lingered behind a few extra seconds.

"I honestly don't know what I'm going to play," Nick pleaded one last time to no one in particular.

As he walked past, Jeff slapped him on the back, a little harder than a typical attaboy. Nick looked back at him. There was a sadness in his eyes. Was it an acknowledgment of how wrong he was? Was it the sad realization that this friendship was over? Screw him. Nick was only upset because he was caught. And did he really think he wouldn't be?

"Rape Me" was about to be a complete disaster. Jeff knew it. Nick really knew it. Chris would soon know it. For the briefest of seconds Jeff felt a twinge of guilt about forcing the band towards this decision. Honestly, they'd recover. One bad song in a high-profile show wouldn't make them or break them. And Jeff would never want to break them. Four of the five were true friends who would never hook up with the girl you just told them you were madly in love with. Nick was about to feel embarrassment on stage. A feeling he had never felt before. He would always know Jeff was responsible for that.

Jeff watched from the wings as Chris stepped up to the mic. He suddenly looked unsure of himself.

"We love you Kurt! This one's for Kurt! We love you!"

Without playing a single note, this was already awkward. Nevertheless, the crowd let out a huge cheer. Then the music started.

Nick pounded on the keyboard, directionless. Bobby couldn't find the beat. Donnie and Sean tried to hit the same riff. It didn't sound like "Rape Me" at all. It was a mess. The audience was confused, trying to figure out if this was a Nirvana song or some awful new Freaks song. Then came the part where Chris was supposed to sing. He couldn't. The words had left his brain completely. Chris began to mumble. He couldn't even say the words "rape me" clearly— surprising, since it was, after all, the title of the song. It sounded more like they were making fun of Nirvana than paying tribute. The crowd began to groan. How long before they abandoned the song? Could they really see it through?

Jeff didn't need to stay and find out. Before walking away he took a last look at Nick. He'd stopped playing completely. He just stood there, beet red from shame. Why didn't he feel that same shame for stabbing a friend in the back? Jeff would have to settle for this. His work here was done.

Jackie

Skanking is a pretty basic dance. Even if you only had a modicum of rhythm you could do it. First step, kick your feet to the beat. The second step is to bend your elbows and ball up your fists, like you're about to throw a punch. Finally, swing your arms along with your feet. The only part that takes any coordination is to make sure when you kick your left leg, you swing your right arm and when you kick your right leg, you swing your left arm. Congratulations, you're now skanking. Whenever a new song starts, it often takes a minute to watch all the dancers find the beat. Jackie's favorite were songs that started off slow and then suddenly got faster and faster. Watching awkward teens trying to adjust and keep up with the music was always funny to her. She also found the dance silly and fun. It'd be a big win if she could get Sean to skank with her.

Sean Greco was off the Stony Brook campus. A personal victory for Jackie. He was at a show and was going to meet her friends. Another victory. The mixtape, however, was a big loss. It was hard for Jackie to believe how simple-minded Sean had been when it came to his musical taste. Was he this closed off to other new experiences too? Food-wise they basically only ate from the campus commissary, mostly so Sean could put it on his student account. Jackie wanted to try Thai food one night but relented when she saw Sean grimace at the thought. They ended up at a White Castle instead. Or there was the time she wanted to watch *Jurassic Park*, easily Jackie's favorite film of last year, but he thought it was just dumb commercialized children's garbage. Instead, on a recommendation from a professor, he made her watch *Stranger Than Paradise*, and then fell asleep five minutes into it. Who didn't like *Jurassic Park*? Who doesn't like dinosaurs? If dinosaurs are kid's stuff then maybe Jackie was a kid. Everyone knows dinosaurs are fucking awesome. Why hadn't she noticed this major red flag?

The streets of Huntington were packed. The sun had set and the air was starting to get cold, but the collective body heat kept the crowd comfortable. A stage had been constructed in the center of town, and lovers of music, as young as eight and as old as sixty, surrounded it. They were all there to see The Scofflaws, a hometown band done good, but it felt like something more. The events of the day had everyone thinking about music and what it meant to them in a way it hadn't the day before. At least a third of these people had probably been on the fence about coming out tonight, and then Kurt happened. Now they needed to be embraced in a community of music. They needed to see up-and-coming bands. Maybe they'd see the next Nirvana. Maybe that would be The Freaks.

The Freaks were one of four local bands opening for The Scofflaws. The other three were straight ska, complete with a horn section. They were older, too. College age. The Freaks were different. They were all still in high school. Their music was more of a ska/punk hybrid. A lot of local ska purists felt they leaned into the punk a little too hard. That only made Jackie like them more. They refused to be defined and thus became embraced by both scenes. A few months ago Jackie had gone to see them play at an emo show in Sunken Meadow State Park, which was immediately following a punk show. Some punk kids stuck around, and when the emo kids arrived the two cliques began to clash. Bottles and punches were thrown. Then The Freaks came on and suddenly the anger stopped. Both groups loved what they were hearing. This was a band all could agree on. This is what makes music special.

The band consisted of five members. Donnie the bassist and Bobby the drummer were brothers who went to Commack High

School. Finding a quality drummer always seemed to be the bane of every local band's existence. So Donnie forced his little brother, who was only in eighth grade at the time, to learn the drums just so The Freaks wouldn't have to worry. The lead singer, Chris, also went to Commack. He couldn't play an instrument, but luckily his stage presence made up for it. It wasn't always this way. At early shows Chris would turn his back to the audience while performing. He was too nervous to look out into the crowd. After about half a dozen shows, his confidence level was high enough that he decided to finally turn around. In the front row was a Rude Girl goddess. Short bob haircut, checkerboard dress and clunky Doc Martens. They've been dating ever since and plan to marry after high school. Jackie was genuinely happy for them.

The lead guitarist was from Smithtown. He was also named Sean and Jackie had also dated him. This Sean, like Jeff, was another nice-enough guy that just didn't work out. Jackie was so infatuated with hanging out with a band all the time, she hadn't noticed how boring he was. How could someone rock so hard on stage and then be so dull? Guitarist Sean only wanted to drive around listening to music, talking about music and making music. It became too repetitive for Jackie. Kind of like only smoking pot and hanging out in a dorm room had.

Finally there was Nick LeWinter, the keyboardist and so called "ladies man." Jackie didn't get the appeal. I mean, she fucked him a few times in the back of his van after shows, but why? She was often overheard saying that he looked like a retarded Muppet. People claimed his luck with ladies had something to do with pheromones, which made as much sense as anything. Nick was confident and Nick was talented. He wrote most of the music, while Chris handled the lyrics. Whether or not The Freaks made it, Nick clearly had a future as a musician. Maybe that's why everyone was so willing to fuck him. Jackie had decided to keep her history with guitarist Sean and Nick a secret from college Sean. Not out of shame or anything. Why flaunt all the guys you've been with in another man's face?

By the time they found parking and made their way to a spot they could see the stage from, The Freaks were starting their second song. Jackie hadn't recognized the first song. Immediately she began moving with the crowd. Skanking. After a minute or so she looked up at Sean, a smile stretched across her face. He wasn't moving.

"Come on!"

Jackie motioned for him to start dancing. She even grabbed his arms and tried to move them to the beat. Sean wasn't having any of it.

"Not my thing, babe." Sean appeared to be the only one not having a good time. He looked down at Jackie. "Everyone looks stupid."

"Of course we do. We're dancing." She was not going to let this kind of negativity ruin her good time.

"I'm gonna find a bathroom." With that he pushed his way out of the crowd and onto the sidewalk. What was his deal? Why wouldn't he just let go and dance? It couldn't be the kid thing anymore. There were people twice his age in the crowd. Jackie kept dancing but she just couldn't shake it. Sean had really put a damper on her fun.

Before she knew it The Freaks set was over. The crowd roared with applause you could hear throughout all of Huntington. Had it already been a half hour? Jackie had totally zoned out on the band's big moment. And where was Sean? Did he go home? No, he wouldn't leave her. Would he?

Finally, peering through the crowd she saw him. He was leaning against a payphone, finishing a slice of pizza. Sean did come to the show, but he hadn't really been with her. Could Jackie still chalk this one up as a win? She wasn't going to cause a scene or call him out. He hated anger, so she'd kill him with positivity.

"What'd you think? Pretty great, right?" she asked, bounding over to him.

"Not my thing," Sean coolly replied.

"Well, thank you for giving it a chance." Jackie tried to hide the sarcasm in her statement. Think positive.

"Anything for you," he said in all seriousness. She went to kiss him but Sean backed off. "Babe. I'm not really down with public displays of affection."

Jackie forced a smile. "Why don't we try and find some of my friends before the next band starts?"

"There's another band?" Sean sounded stunned, as if he'd never been to a show before.

"There's four more, including The Scofflaws." Sean looked beside himself. "We're not going to stay for all of them," she continued. "We have to get to the party."

Before Sean could protest, Jackie grabbed his hand and dragged him through the crowd. The Freaks were packing up their equipment. Jackie climbed up on the stage. Sean reluctantly followed. Immediately she threw her arms around Chris.

"You were so fucking great!" she exclaimed.

"Thanks," Chris said. "Thanks so much for coming. It was a pretty shaky start, but I think we recovered and the crowd seemed into it. I was just talking to a guy who wants us to perform next week in a battle of the bands at Da Funky Phish."

"I'll be there." Jackie attempted to transition. "Chis, this is my boyfriend, Sean."

Chris extended his hand. "Nice to meet you, man. Thanks for coming out."

"Yeah." Other than a half-assed handshake, that's all Sean would give him. Yeah.

"O.k.," Chris said, breaking an awkward silence. "I have to get the rest of the equipment out of here. Going to Sage's later?"

"You know it!" It was becoming harder and harder for Jackie to keep this positive smile plastered on her face. Sean was just being rude. They made their way over to Nick, who was packing up his two keyboards. "Great show!"

Nick turned to Jackie. He seemed a little off. Startled. Distracted.

"Oh, hey Jackie," he said.

"This is Sean."

"Another Sean, huh?" Nick extended his hand.

"What's that mean?" Sean snapped. Nick pulled his hand away.

"Nothing. She just recently dated another dude named Sean is all."

Jackie kept up the smile and decided to change the subject. "Have you seen Jeff or Seth or any of those guys around?"

"Seth, no. But Jeff is around here somewhere." Nick nervously peered out into the crowd, looking for him. "Listen, I'll catch up with you later." Abruptly, Nick pushed past them and headed down from the stage.

"Shit," Jackie said. "I really wanted you to meet Jeff. He'll be at the party though."

"Who's this other Sean?" college Sean asked.

"What?"

"You dated some other guy named Sean."

The events of the evening had proven that this Sean didn't even like Jackie that much. So why was he being all alpha male? God, men can be so fucking pathetic.

"Actually, I dated two other guys named Sean. You're number three. I collect Seans." This was true. The part about dating two other Seans, not the collecting thing. Sean's eyes widened. Jackie had to do more than smile to defuse this.

"Why don't you and I skip the rest of the show, go over to the Dix Hills Diner and grab a bite before the party?"

"I already had a slice."

"You could get dessert. Or just watch me eat."

He thought about it. "Sure. I'll probably smoke in the car, so I'll get the munchies again."

They stepped down from the stage and started moving through the crowd, back towards the car. Jackie was still smiling, but on the inside she was frustrated. It had been a day of standing up for things she believed in and now she was being a total submissive. Needle him, just a little.

"Hey," Jackie said. "Why didn't you like *Jurassic Park* again?"

"I never saw it," Sean said.

"Wait, really?"

"No interest."

"I know it's a big Hollywood movie and you hate that, but it's really good. The dinosaurs look so real. And it's suspenseful. There's a scene where a T-Rex is—"

"It's propaganda," he interrupted.

"Propaganda? For what? Science? DNA? A shirtless Jeff Goldblum?"

"Dinosaurs aren't real."

What. The. Fuck. This was crazier than his ideas on female singers or black vaginas. Jackie laughed. He must be joking.

"I'm serious," Sean doubled down. "Dinosaurs aren't real."

Jackie looked around, mortified. She was sure people were watching them. Judging. She took his hand and tried to get him to stop. He didn't.

"Why do you believe dinosaurs are real? Because some man who works at a museum says so? Why were no dinosaur bones discovered before the 1800s? If there were so many dinosaurs, wouldn't we be finding bones all the time in our backyards? And why would a meteor kill all the dinosaurs who lived in the ocean? I get the ones on land, but the *ocean*? Plus the laws of physics and gravity prevent creatures that large from actually walking the earth. Dinosaurs were created to help the struggling museum industry, later the toy industry and now the film industry. You're so naïve about the world, babe. It's kinda cute."

Jackie didn't know what to say. Of all the things she thought she'd have to stand up for today, dinosaurs were not one of them.

Matt

"I've been trying to call you for an hour," Matt complained into the phone.

It had probably been more like a half hour. Maybe even fifteen minutes. Matt was frustrated and finally relieved to get something other than a busy signal on Tariq's line.

"I was using the Internet," Tariq responded. Matt didn't really understand what that was. He knew it was a place you could go on your computer to talk to people or share information, but that was the extent of his knowledge. How did it work? Was the Internet a physical thing? Matt didn't even own a computer. In fact, Tariq was his only friend who did and occasionally he went onto the Internet. This would drive Matt insane since it would tie up Tariq's phone line and make it impossible to get in touch with him. If those busy signals were any indication it seemed like he was spending more and more time on the computer.

"Aren't you supposed to be having sex right now?" Tariq asked.

"Rebecca got sick. She couldn't make it," Matt lied.

"That sucks."

"So what do you want to do tonight?"

"I was thinking of going to Sage's party," Tariq said.

"Nah, I'm not feeling that. It's been a weird day. You want to rent a movie?" There was a long pause on the other end of the phone. Matt continued, "With the whole Kurt Cobain thing I bet the party is more like a funeral. Who needs that? Hey, do you know what Kurt Cobain's favorite movie was?"

"No. What was it?"

"I'm asking you."

"Why would I know?"

"We should find out and rent it as a tribute."

"I can probably find out on the Internet," Tariq said. "Kurt's been a big topic in the chat rooms."

'What's a chat room?" Matt asked.

"It's, I don't know, you just talk to people in it." Tariq was getting flustered. He clearly didn't know how to explain it or just didn't want to. Either way Matt let it go.

"O.k. Check it out and then come get me."

"Alright." Tariq hung up.

Matt had about a half hour until Tariq got there. Shit, that meant a half hour with no distractions. To be left alone with his own thoughts. Would he tell Tariq the truth about what happened? Talking it out with someone might help Matt better understand it. How do you tell all the guys that you rejected a woman who wanted to fuck you in order to keep watching a film you've seen one hundred times before? None of them knew Rebecca, so none of them ever had to know the truth. Hell, maybe Matt would just lie and just tell everyone he had sex. That way his virginity would no longer be an issue.

To pass the time Matt decided to read the latest issue of Entertainment Weekly and put on some music. The *Reservoir Dogs* soundtrack was already in his CD player.

Matt never crunched the numbers but he'd guess eighty-five percent of his CDs were movie scores and soundtracks. Film just meant more to him than music. And he loved being able to identify a song with a film. Right now hearing "Hooked on a Feeling" made him think about the exact moment it was used in *Reservoir Dogs*. Maybe he should have just kept watching the video? No, he needed to get out into the world. Forget about whatever had happened. Or what hadn't happened. The song was now reminding him of his humiliation. Does that mean *Reservoir Dogs* would now remind him of being humiliated? Had he ruined one of his favorite movies? Impossible...*right*?

Matt decided to switch CDs. The brilliant opening notes of the *Jurassic Park* soundtrack began to play. He was already getting goosebumps from it. Was there anyone better than John Williams?

Suddenly the phone rang.

"Hello."

"*Over the Edge*." The voice was Tariq's. Why was he calling instead of being on his way over?

"What?" Matt asked confused.

"*Over the Edge*. That was Kurt's favorite movie."

Matt had never heard of it. Could he, the cinephile that he was, admit to such a thing? Maybe split the difference.

"I've *heard* of it, but never *seen* it. What's it about again?"

"A bunch of kids who rebel and take over some private community."

"Right. Very 'Smells Like Teen Spirt.'"

"Matt Dillon's in it," Tariq added.

"You're amazing with that computer. You're like Matthew Broderick in *War Games*."

Silence.

"Global Thermonuclear War," Matt said in his best computer voice.

More silence from Tariq.

"So get over here and we'll go rent it."

"Alright," Tariq said as he finally hung up.

What's wrong with him? Just relay that information when you get here. Why call?

The phone was still in Matt's hand. Should he call Rebecca? It still wasn't too late to apologize. Tell her he doesn't know what came over him. Ask for a second chance. Beyond the possibility of staying with her, didn't Rebecca deserve an explanation, even if the explanation lacked an explainable reason?

Matt stared at the phone contemplating this for what felt like forever, all while music about sick triceratops played in the background. And before he knew it, Tariq was pulling into the driveway.

Oh well. It seemed Matt had missed his moment.

T.J.

The opening guitar riff was unmistakable, followed by a welcoming "*Cha!*"

Multicolored neon lights lit up the normally dull-looking bowling alley and music blared, transforming it into the lamest suburban club on Long Island. High school kids couldn't go to bars or dance clubs so instead they would often come here. Most of them wouldn't even bowl. They'd just dance, letting loose to a selection of music that ran the gamut from the very fitting Guns N' Roses to not-really-rocking Debbie Gibson. Maybe it was a lame excuse for a club, but it was their lame excuse for a club.

A few members of the group actually did enjoy bowling. Matt, for example, one night got a "turkey." Given he'd never been good enough to get three strikes in a row before, everyone thought it was a fluke. Everyone except Matt. Inspired, in his junior year he went all in on bowling. He even bought his own ball that he'd lug along to Rock N Bowl. But the harder he tried, the worse he got. The one benefit to Matt's hopelessness was that he had befriended Evan, the friendly college student who worked behind the counter handing out shoes. As long as his boss wasn't around, Evan would always waive the shoe rental charge for Matt's friends.

T.J. and Liz walked in as if they were on a mission. They were high on yodeling and a budding romance and maybe still weed. T.J. remembered a scene in *Goodfellas* where the gangster was bringing his girlfriend to some club. To impress her, the gangster walked in through the back entrance, bypassing the line and getting a table right in front of the stage. T.J. remembered this scene so well because Jeff and Matt watched it over and over, droning on about how it was all one take and wondering how they could

133

recreate the lighting for a short video they were making. For the first time listening to them drone on about film was becoming useful. T.J. had an in at this "club" and he was going to use it to impress Liz.

He motioned for her to follow him. There was a small line of people, but T.J. was not going to wait. Evan was standing behind the counter, spraying Dr. Scholl's out of an aerosol can into recently worn shoes.

"Evan! What's up man?" T.J. said in an overly familiar fashion.

"Hey..."

It was obvious to T.J. that Evan recognized him but couldn't place the name. As long as he didn't mention that, T.J. was fine with it. He didn't want to appear unmemorable in front of Liz.

"So, um, we're looking to bowl, and...." T.J. was having trouble figuring out how to ask for a hookup. "...And is there an open lane?"

Evan looked at the line of people being helped by his co-workers. Then he peered down at the lanes, most of which were being used. He smiled.

"I think I could hook you up on twenty-seven."

"Awesome." T.J. reached for his wallet. Evan shook him off.

"Pay me after. Otherwise they'll notice I let you cut the line."

T.J. motioned towards Liz trying to gauge her reaction to this impressive display of respect he was getting at the Smithtown bowling alley. She didn't seem to notice.

"Shoe size?" Evan asked.

"Ten and a half," T.J. answered as he started the arduous process of unlacing his Doc Martens. Evan waved him off.

"Don't worry about that," Evan said. The special treatment for T.J. was just getting better. Clearly at this bowling alley Liz would see he was a man who was respected. Evan turned to Liz.

"Eight," she replied. Evan smiled.

"I have a brand-new pair of women's size eight, never been worn." He reached below the counter and pulled out a shiny pair of bowling shoes. No scuff marks. No stinky smell of a thousand fungus-infested feet. What unbelievable luck T.J. was having! He was a bigwig at the bowling alley. What's next? Maybe he could get some comped chicken fingers or sodas? That'd probably be pushing it. Probably.

*****

They were in the middle of their first game. Liz was rolling gutter ball after gutter ball, and was clearly frustrated by it. T.J. on the other hand was bowling the best game of his life. He wanted to impress Liz, show her he was good at something, and she'd have to be impressed with the skill T.J. was showcasing. A clattering of pins exploded over the sounds of Madonna expressing herself. This was another music video T.J. often jerked off to, always trying to time his orgasm to the sequence where Madonna is in chains. The thought of sex coupled with the adrenaline of the great game he was bowling made for a potent combination. Tonight, T.J. could do anything.

"So, it's just bowling in the dark with music?"

That's exactly as T.J. described it, but clearly Liz still expected something more. He had been so wrapped up in his own ego he hadn't realized just how bored Liz was. It was her turn to roll and T.J. noticed that crazed gleam in her eye. She was sick of gutter balls and probably sick of bowling in general.

Holding the ball with both hands she suddenly started running up the lane screaming. It was slippery and she slid a little in her brand-new shoes, but she made it halfway to the pins before heaving the ball towards them with all her might. The ball hit the wood with a thud and barreled towards the pins. Crash! Eight down, her best score yet.

As she slipped and slid back towards T.J., he looked nervous. Normally he was all for breaking the rules of bowling and society, but Evan had done him a favor and he didn't want to piss him off.

Too late.

"Hey!" Evan yelled. "You can't go past the line!"

T.J. politely waved to Evan. A sorry without saying sorry. He didn't want to go against anything Liz wanted but he also needed to make sure things were smoothed over with the bowling gods. Evan sent an annoyed glance back at T.J. before returning to his shoe spraying.

"What did that prick say?" Liz asked. As she took her last step off the lane, onto the more normal surface, she slipped, falling right into T.J.'s arms. They both laughed and regained their footing. Evan's scorn was worth it.

"He was just saying you can't run up the lane."

"Lame."

"Right?" T.J. agreed.

"I mean isn't this called Rock N Bowl? It should be fucking crazy! A free-for-all," Liz said.

Liz's ball came back up the chute. She still had two pins to deal with. T.J. looked worried. He didn't want her to run up the lane again, but he wouldn't stop her if she did. Liz reared back, her thin fingers barely able to hold the weight of the ball. She let it fly…into the neighboring lane.

It could have easily been an accident, but the glee Liz took in her actions quickly made T.J. realize this was her plan.

Her ball sailed into the gutter of the next lane.

"What the fuck?" The tough guy using that lane was clearly not happy. Neither was the cute brunette with him, whom he was trying to be a big man in front of. It looked like they were on a date too. *Was this a date?*

"Sorry," T.J. somewhat genuinely replied.

"Yeah, sorry," Liz seconded, much less genuinely. The tough guy went back to his game. "Why don't we go," Liz said to T.J.

"Whatever you want." Shit, T.J. He shouldn't have said that. Women want you to do whatever they want but not actually tell them you'll do whatever they want. This was at least T.J.'s theory. Unless of course they had no interest in fucking you, in that case you could tell them you'd do whatever they wanted to and it wouldn't matter. Unless, of course, they only didn't want to fuck you because you said you'd do whatever they wanted to in the first place. It was a frustrating cycle with no easy answers. Thoughts like this went through T.J.'s head constantly.

T.J. started to kick off his bowling shoes.

"Let's steal them," Liz said.

"The shoes?" T.J. asked.

"How swiss would it be for me to walk around every day in awesome new bowling shoes?"

In that moment two things were clear. The first was that they couldn't steal the shoes. It would be a betrayal to Evan, who had hooked him up, but more importantly to all his friends who hung out there. Not only could T.J. never return, but gone would be the days of free shoe rentals for all.

The second was that they were definitely going to steal the shoes.

"Let's do it," he said.

"Should we just make a run for it or just walk out all casual?" Liz sounded really excited, as if they were robbing Fort Knox. T.J. smiled playfully, and bolted for the door as fast as he could.

"Asshole," Liz said through laughter. She raced after him. T.J. once again had the upper hand. She might have suggested stealing the shoes, but he was the one who ran. The one who forced them to actually do it.

They pushed past patrons, through the doors and into the parking lot. Without looking back, they raced towards the car. T.J. was heading towards the passenger's side to unlock Liz's door, like a gentleman would. But when pulling a heist it's crucial for the driver to get in first. Scrambling for the keys, T.J. changed course for the driver's side and jumped in. As he reached over to unlock her door, he could see Evan racing towards them.

"Hurry!" Liz exclaimed.

T.J. pulled up her lock and she jumped inside. As he started the car, Liz furiously began rolling down the window. Evan was almost there, screaming "Stop! Stop!"

Still not totally used to Seth's car, T.J. awkwardly backed out of the parking space, actually headed towards Evan. As he threw it in drive to pull away, Evan reached them.

"Yodelayheehoo!"

Liz let a Yodel fly directly into Evan's face. Startled, he jumped back, wiping the cream from his eyes. Yup, T.J could never come back here.

As cruel as Liz was, she was exciting. Maybe T.J. would pay for these actions in the long run, but right now the thrill was worth it. How cruel was it really? So they stole some bowling shoes and got Drake's Cakes on some passersby. Victimless crimes. And really, wasn't this something he started when he threw that first Sunny Doodle? If T.J. complained, wouldn't he be a hypocrite?

"Oh my God! What should we do now?" Liz was physically shaking from the excitement. Since her time in the clinic, it was obvious she hadn't gotten out much.

"Are you hungry?" T.J. asked.

"It's Friday. Is there a Carvel around here?" she asked.

On Fridays Carvel ran a special, buy one eight-ounce sundae, get a second free. This date continued to be full of great deals. T.J. headed towards the ice cream shop.

They pulled into the Carvel parking lot, and before T.J. had even come to a complete stop, Liz was out of the car, racing inside.

Few things made him feel like a kid again more than trips to Carvel. When he was a child, every year his mom would buy him a Cookie Puss ice cream cake. As is the Cookie Puss tradition, his first move would be to rip off the ice cream cone nose and eat it. When he was fourteen he told his mom to stop buying Cookie Puss for his birthday, that it was kid's stuff. Secretly he still wanted one every year. Should he confess this to Liz? If he told her about the nostalgia he had for ice cream cake, maybe they could buy one and eat it together? They'd never finish, but maybe it would bond them in some disgusting, bloated but beautiful way. Forget it. Cookie Puss was too expensive. They were about to buy two-for-one sundaes.

Liz ran up to the woman behind the counter.

"Rather than get two-for-one sundaes, can I get them combined into one large sundae?" Liz asked.

It would appear T.J. wasn't getting a two-for-one deal after all.

"I guess so," the employee said. She looked tired, someone not in the mood to play games. Liz was the last customer she wanted to deal with.

"I'll have a vanilla sundae with hot fudge and rainbow sprinkles," Liz ordered. The woman got right on it, filling up a larger than eight-ounce cup full of soft serve. Liz gave T.J. a wink; she was up to something. On dripped the hot fudge, followed by the pouring of sprinkles. She handed Liz the sundae.

"What's this?" Liz questioned.

"Your sundae."

"What size cup is that?"

The haggard employee looked down at it. "Fourteen-ounce."

"What the fuck?" Liz shouted. "I asked for my two eight-ounce sundaes to be combined. That would be sixteen ounces. Where are my other two ounces?"

T.J. knew this was bullshit. Liz knew this was bullshit. The Carvel employee certainly knew this was bullshit. Technically however, it was correct. After letting out the sigh of a woman who just wanted her shift to end already, the employee started making a whole new sundae. Since there were no sixteen-ounce cups, this time she put it in a twenty-ounce cup, giving Liz a well-earned four extra ounces.

"I'll also get caramel and chocolate chips," Liz said.

"Additional toppings are fifty cents each," the Carvel employee replied.

"But this is two sundaes combined. So I get four toppings. *Remember?*"

It was becoming clear that Liz might actually be some kind of jerk. T.J. ignored this fact and ordered himself a chocolate shake.

Jackie

Was it possible that in the past three months Jackie and Sean had never had an actual conversation? Because Jackie had invested so little into whatever was going on between them, she hadn't realized how insane he was. All their conversations had been surface level. Sure, he had said he didn't like *Jurassic Park*, but she had never bothered to ask why. Jackie accepted it because she didn't want anything more than a hot older guy to fool around with. The three months had flown by. It was easy to blame herself. Not for being blind to who Sean really was, but for actually finally opening up her eyes. It would have been better to leave well enough alone, never leave the dorm and never know how much of a dumb fuck her boyfriend is.

And mean. Why was he being rude to her friends? Jackie couldn't bring this prick to Sage's party. She also didn't want to give him an out on principle. He owed it to her to go. Jackie deserved it.

They sat in a booth at the Dix Hills Diner. Since the dinosaur discussion they had barely said two words to each other. She picked at her French fries and slowly sipped a vanilla Coke. Sean had already inhaled a piece of chocolate pie, because, as predicted, he got high on the car ride over. Each booth featured a mini jukebox, and Sean was slowly flipping through it. They mostly featured oldies like Elvis or The Beach Boys. What classic female artist could Jackie play to annoy him?

Across the diner she noticed Adam Grasso and Marie Rossanda. Both of them had graduated from Smithtown a year earlier. They now attended Suffolk Community College, which despite having a really good reputation, was unaffectionately referred to as "Scruffic." Marie was into anime and always dressed in obnoxiously bright clothing that popped. She was also skeletally thin. Seth told Jackie that shortly after high school Marie developed a bad heroin habit and now had hepatitis. Adam was perpetually wearing his father's old army jacket. He was also perpetually following Marie around. Adam had been by her side for years. Jackie felt bad for him. Hepatitis or not, it was never going to happen.

Jackie pulled out a quarter and put it in the jukebox. She selected B3. It wasn't an oldie. In fact, it was a song from an era Sean should appreciate and an artist from only a few towns over.

Sean rolled his eyes. "I know what you're doing."

"Things were too quiet," Jackie said.

"Pat Benatar? You don't like Pat Benatar."

"I *love* Pat Benatar," Jackie said. "I love all 'chick' singers. It's male singers I can't stand. They're all so whiny, singing about feelings and emotions. A bunch of pussies. Act like a goddamn man."

"Funny."

After tonight Jackie could never kiss Sean again. Certainly never sleep with him again. Just get through tonight and disappear on him. He won't mind. He and Donna could go down on each other in between publishing zines about how dinosaurs are a myth. But the whole thing was so confusing. Jackie didn't know what she wanted or what she expected. Fuck and run.

"Why didn't you give my mixtape a chance? I made it for you. I put time and thought into it."

Sean sighed. "Babe, you realize this isn't really a thing, right? Like, we don't have a future. And it scares me to see you so invested."

Stunned silence. How did Sean not realize that Jackie already knew this? He was about to end it and she hated how much that hurt.

"I know but—"

"I mean you're hot," he continued, "and I have fun with you. But then you want me to meet your friends…."

Jackie wasn't going to fight for this garbage pile of a quote unquote relationship, but she didn't want Sean to leave thinking she was an unrealistic high school kid. She tried to interject.

"That's just something people do. When you like someone, even as just a friend, you want them to meet—"

"See? 'Like.' You *like* me. That's a lot of pressure."

Jackie wasn't raising her voice. She was too busy trying to understand.

"But you page me 143 all the time and—"

"And you shouldn't be pouring so much into some dumb mixtape…."

"I thought it might inspire—"

"…with that awful Tori Amos."

Suddenly the sadness and confusion stopped. Jackie now saw red. As red as Tori's beautiful hair.

"Tori Amos is a goddamn hero!" Jackie shouted.

"Because she was raped?"

"Because she overcame it," she stated proudly. "Because she found a place of inner strength and turned pain into song. Because she spoke out about it, letting other women know they're not alone."

"See, and because of that she has high school girls thinking she's some great musician," Sean said. "It's all marketing. I wouldn't be surprised if she lied about her rape."

Enough.

"Women and men of all ages think she's a great musician because no one plays piano like her, no one writes meaningful songs like her, and despite your tone-deaf ears I assure you no one sings like her! She is a fucking goddess whose name doesn't deserve to be spoken across your lips. You're a retarded piece of shit! You know that, right? You're just some big dumb fuck who doesn't know anything about music or dinosaurs or what's going on in the mind of a woman! Fuck off you dickless...dickhead!"

Jackie could have used a more clever phrase than "dickless dickhead" but in times of true anger this is the best most of us can muster. Other than that, she beamed with pride, feeling really good about herself. Somewhere during the argument Jackie had stood up. The entire diner was staring at her now, including Adam and Marie, who were clearly holding back nervous laughter. They all sat quietly, awaiting her next move. Jackie needed to make a bigger statement than this. She was now the one carrying the collective pain of every woman scorned. Love, of course, is a battlefield.

Jackie picked up her vanilla Coke and threw it in Sean's face. Gasps from the "audience." Adam let out a Nelson Muntz-style

"Ha ha." Sean looked humiliated. He probably wanted to hit her. Good. Let him try. She marched away from the table confidently, owning what just happened. Sean began to scream at her.

"That's a high school girl for ya! Immature babies all of them."

Jackie didn't turn around. Instead she headed towards Adam and Marie's table.

"I fucked Donna," Sean continued to yell. "I fucked her today!"

Did he really think that would hurt her? Jackie stood over Adam and Marie. They looked at her in awe.

"Can you guys give me a lift?"

Jackie had never really known what she wanted out of dating Sean Greco. Maybe one day she'd be able to explain it. Maybe one day she'd be able to explain him. Right now, she was just glad it was over.

Matt

There was so much trash on the car's floor that when you sat down, your knees were level with your chest. Matt's feet crunched on what was mostly old fast food wrappers and cups. Tariq shared this tiny, beat-up Toyota with his mother. Why would she let the car get this dirty? Where were the demands for Tariq to clean it up? Could an adult really be this filthy?

Tariq pulled out of the driveway. Matt tried his best to make himself comfortable.

"Which Blockbuster?" Tariq asked.

"Let's try the Hauppauge one," Matt replied. "It's bigger."

They drove for about two blocks in silence before Matt decided to speak again.

"Yeah, it's too bad Rebecca couldn't come out tonight. I was really looking forward to, well, you know."

"She was sick?" Tariq questioned.

"Strep throat she thinks."

"That's pretty contagious." As Tariq said this he leaned away from Matt, ever so slightly.

"I was thinking and I don't think it's going to work out between us." Tariq subtly moved back into his original positon, continuing to listen to Matt. "I mean, I'd love it to. She's gorgeous. But let's face it, come September we'll both be at different schools, hundreds of miles away. It would never work even if I wanted it to. At most this relationship will be a fuck and run."

"So you're going to fuck her and then dump her?" Tariq questioned.

"What? No. I mean eventually yes I guess but—"

"That seems shitty." Even though Tariq's tone never changed, it felt like he was judging Matt.

"I'm not going to fuck her and then immediately be like, 'so long.' I mean, I *assume* we'll date for a while but eventually it can't last."

"Why not?"

"Because of distance."

"You don't know that," Tariq pointed out. "Maybe you'll love each other and find a way to make it work."

"Relationships are complicated things, Tariq. You've never been in one."

"*You've* never been in one," Tariq countered.

"What do you call what I'm in now?"

"I think if you like someone you find a way to make it work. Life finds a way."

Matt never realized Tariq was a secret romantic. This conversation was getting really annoying. It was completely pointless for reasons Matt wasn't willing to explain. Then, he noticed a manila folder crammed between the seats. Matt pulled it out. Snooping as a distraction. He opened it up. A series of photographs fell into his lap. They were of mixed quality. Some images blurry and grainy, some sharp. Instead of glossy magazine paper, these photos were on computer paper. Dozens of photos. Dozens of photos of Winona Ryder.

"Hey!" Tariq shouted. "Put that back."

"What the hell is this? Where did you get all these photos?"

There were still images of Winona from nearly all her films. *Reality Bites. Dracula. Edward Scissorhands. Beetlejuice. Heathers.* Even *The Age of Innocence.*

"Why do you have all these?" Matt asked, totally confused.

"I like Winona Ryder. She's my number-one celebrity crush. You know that."

"And what are you doing with a million photos of her?"

"I don't know. I found photos on the Internet and started printing them out." Tariq was clearly embarrassed. Matt should probably just drop the subject. Nah, continue. Anything to take the heat off himself.

"So you collect them? Are you making an album?"

"I don't know."

"Do you jerk off to them?"

"Put them away," Tariq protested without answering the question.

"Because I would. I would rub my dick all over them. How very!" Matt held up a particularly adorable image of Winona from *Heathers.* Tariq began reaching over and snagging the photos back, shoving them in the folder, all while trying to keep an eye on the road.

"You know, Winona was my first celebrity crush too," Matt continued. "Well, more specifically Lydia Deetz, the character she played in *Beetlejuice*. She was so dark and weird, but in a really approachable way, you know?"

Tariq said nothing.

This statement was mostly true. Winona was definitely in the top five, and that certainly felt good enough to justify what Matt had said. If a gun was put to his head and he had to answer honestly, he'd probably say Madonna was his earliest celebrity crush. Or maybe Carrie Fisher in *Return of the Jedi*. The first time he remembered sexualizing a woman was Beverly D'Angelo. In the film *Vacation* she had a totally gratuitous but very much appreciated topless scene. It was the first time Matt had ever seen bare breasts, and the memory was seared in his brain. Had it occurred to Matt that he'd just blown an opportunity to see breasts in real life? He had really screwed this night up.

Matt looked over at Tariq. His eyes widened. In the darkness, he hadn't noticed it until now.

"You're still wearing your *X-Files* shirt?!?"

"So are you," Tariq replied.

"We're going to look like retards. We're going to look like retarded homos."

"I thought you'd change for your date."

"Fuck! I can't believe we're going to walk around dressed like this."

*****

Matt could waste all day wandering around Blockbuster Video. It was probably his favorite place on Earth.

WPIX, a local television channel, was known primarily for airing Yankees games. This didn't interest Matt. What did interest him was when the Yankees weren't playing, they'd almost exclusively air movies. Movies of all sorts. Everything from contemporary fare like *Die Hard* to older classics like *Bonnie and Clyde*. On Saturday afternoons they would air one movie after another after another, and as a child Matt would park himself in front of the television, taking in whatever was on. It didn't matter if it was a Clint Eastwood Western or an Oscar-winning musical, Matt wanted to see them all. His father would often complain that Matt should be outside, playing a sport or riding bikes with friends. This always seemed hypocritical, since he never had time to have a catch or teach Matt to ride a bike. Matt wasn't exactly sure how his father spent weekend afternoons and didn't care. He'd rather be raised by the warm glow of television.

In 1985 his family finally broke down and bought a VCR. Now Matt could record every film WPIX aired. He didn't care that they were edited for television. They were still telling him powerful stories. Still giving him a way to escape the doldrums of life. And now he could even fast-forward through the commercials.

Soon video stores began popping up all over town. Movieland, USA Video and various mom and pop chains. Matt would beg his mother to bring him to one of these stores every Friday night so he could rent half a dozen films. This would barely be enough to get him through the weekend. By the early nineties Blockbuster Videos were popping up all over Long Island. They had a bigger and better selection than the other stores. Where USA Video might only have four copies of *Batman Returns*, Blockbuster would have forty. And if they didn't have the video you wanted, no need to panic, they could call the other Blockbuster in the next town over and check for you. Matt and Jeff spent many nights going from store to store tracking down hard-to-find films. Typically they'd spend hours walking the aisles, the selections they saw causing deep discussion on how to properly rank the James Bond films (*Goldfinger* at number one, obviously) or who was a scarier slasher, Freddy or Jason (Freddy, he had more personality and even with a crazed killer, personality goes a long way).

Matt and Tariq wandered past the new releases. Shelves devoted to *Dazed and Confused, Demolition Man, The Fugitive*, all films Matt had seen in the theater. As they browsed the selections Matt awkwardly crossed his arms over his chest, trying to hide the matching attire, convinced the customers were staring at their shirts.

"What's your favorite Winona role?" Matt asked Tariq.

"*Heathers.*"

"Mine's *Scissorhands*. It's just such a wonderful fairytale and she's different in it. She's the princess, not the weirdo."

"I thought you liked the weirdo?"

Couldn't Matt like both princesses and weirdos? Why would Tariq question him?

"I guess it would be in drama," Matt suggested. The pair walked through a few aisles making their way to the drama section. *Over the Edge*. **O**. Matt traced his finger along the cassettes but they went right from *The Outsiders* to *Paper Moon*.

"What? How could they not have it?" Matt asked.

"It's not a popular movie. I'd never heard of it," Tariq reminded him.

"It was the favorite film of a cultural icon! A popular man! They should carry it."

Matt looked over the VHS cases again, in case he might have missed something. Of course he hadn't. "Maybe it's in the action section," he said. "You know these stores don't know how to organize anything properly."

They raced over to the action section. **O**. The only action film containing the word 'over' was *Over the Top*. Matt was really annoyed, surprisingly so considering an hour ago he didn't know this film even existed. He slammed an open palm into the side of the shelves in frustration. What else could go wrong tonight?

"Let's ask," Tariq suggested.

As they walked through Action, towards the front of the store, they passed by a display of all three Indiana Jones movies.

"What's the best Spielberg film?" Matt asked.

Without hesitation Tariq responded, "*Jaws*."

"Really?"

"What?"

"I just thought you'd go with *Raiders* or maybe *E.T.*"

"*Jaws*."

"Why?" Matt questioned.

"I don't know. It's his most intense."

"*Jurassic Park* is pretty intense."

"It's just *Jaws* with dinosaurs," Tariq rebutted.

"I'd say *Raiders* is his best. It's the greatest adventure film of all time. It's structured remarkably. How did he not win for that? *Chariots of Fire* can blow me. I wonder when *Schindler's List* comes out on video? I'd love to see it again. *That* could be his masterwork. It's not as much fun as his other stuff but it's so important."

"*The Color Purple* is important," Tariq reminded him.

"Yeah. I guess."

They reached the counter. The long-haired clerk was using a standalone VHS rewinder to rewind the dozens of tapes customers returned without rewinding at home. Matt would never bring back a tape without rewinding it. He would never return a tape late. He respected the rules of the video store. How hard is it to just hit rewind when the movie's over? People were so goddamn lazy.

"Excuse me," Matt said, getting the clerk's attention.

"How can I help you?" The clerk spoke slowly, as if he was really trying to concentrate on the task at hand. He was probably stoned.

"Do you have the movie *Over the Edge*?" Matt asked.

"I've never heard of it," the clerk replied.

"It was Kurt Cobain's favorite film."

The clerk didn't react. He didn't flinch at the name Kurt Cobain. He didn't check the computer database for the video. Matt continued to talk. "Crazy about Kurt, right? With the whole, um, suicide today. It's really sad." The clerk ever so slightly shrugged his shoulders.

Matt looked over at Tariq as if to say "a little help" but Tariq was too busy studying the candy selection. Matt would have to go it alone.

"We wanted to rent *Over the Edge* because I read it was his favorite movie and we thought it might be a fun way to celebrate his life. You know?"

"Why not just listen to his music?" The clerk finally chose to respond, like a smartass.

"I've been listening to his music all day. I was listening to it before I drove here. Now I want to see something that inspired that music. Can you check the computer?"

Matt tried to speak calmly but his tone had become slightly rude. Just do your fucking job. The clerk finally began typing it into the database.

"Nothin', man. Sorry."

"Could you call another store? Smithtown?"

Why did Matt have to tell this guy how to do his job? Jeff worked at the video store in the mall and he would never be this lackadaisical in his job, no matter how mind-numbing. Delivering art to the masses was important.

"Do you guys have *Over the Edge*?" the clerk asked into the phone. "Thanks." And with that he hung up. "They don't have it."

Two seconds, maybe three, had passed in between the time the clerk asked about the film and him hanging up. There was no way they had time to check. Had this long-haired stoner even made the phone call? Call him out. Call him a liar. But how?

"Can you try Commack?" Matt pleaded.

The clerk picked up the phone. Matt watched him dial what he hoped was a real number. Then he immediately hung up.

"It's busy."

Matt had enough of this Blockbuster. He motioned to Tariq, who'd ripped open a bag of Twizzlers and was eating one. "Let's just go to Commack," Matt said. "Hopefully they'll have it."

"I gotta pay for these," Tariq mumbled through a mouth full of red licorice.

As Tariq settled up with the clerk, Matt decided to press his luck and ask another question.

"Hey, let me ask you something. When does *Schindler's List* come out?"

"What's that?" the clerk asked without irony.

"What do you mean?"

"What is it?"

"*What is it?* It just won a shitload of Oscars."

"Never heard of it."

"It's about the Holocaust. It was in black and white."

"Black and white. That sucks."

Matt locked eyes with the clerk. He was getting mad. What was wrong with this guy? How can you work at a video store and not know about the most recent Best Picture winner? How could you be around films all day and not appreciate the beauty of black and white cinematography? This didn't make sense.

"Steven Spielberg's newest film," Matt added.

"Spielberg? Never heard of him."

Matt was apoplectic.

"He's fucking with you," Tariq interrupted, licorice juice spilling down his chin. "Let's go."

Tariq was right, and deep down Matt knew he should let it go. The clerk never smiled. Never gave any indication this was some sort of joke.

"I'm never coming to this Blockbuster again. You got that?"

No reaction to Matt's empty threat. Was the clerk psychotic? Tariq was already headed out the door, but Matt didn't want to leave. He wanted this clerk to understand the kind of man he was dealing with.

"Fuck you! There's no reason to be a dick. I just wanted to rent a fucking movie." With that Matt knocked over a stack of returned tapes that were waiting to be placed back on the shelves. They spilled onto the floor behind the counter. "Have a nice night, asshole!"

The clerk didn't clean up the tapes. He just continued to stare at Matt as he walked into the parking lot, ranting and raving to Tariq or anyone else who would listen.

Jeff

The Katie situation was now even more of a situation.

Jeff had walked far enough away from the show that he could no longer hear The Freaks playing. It was safe to assume they probably righted the ship by now, and all Jeff wanted to remember was Nick floundering on stage. He had to refocus. He had to get in touch with Katie before the night was through. Where was she? From a payphone he tried her home line again. No answer. She was probably out on the town with friends, telling them all about how she just hooked up with Nick outside the Smith Haven Mall. Jeff had no choice but to embark on a complicated and highly convoluted way of contacting the girl of his dreams.

First he would use his prepaid calling card to beep Katie "911" with the payphone number. Then he would wait by the payphone, hoping she'd have access to a phone herself and call back. How long would he wait? As long as it takes. If someone needed to use the phone while he waited, he'd hold the receiver to his ear and pretend he was talking, while pressing his hand down on the base so the phone line stayed open. Then when she called back he'd find out where she was and see if they could meet up. If she couldn't meet up, he'd have to just confess his love to her right here and now. In the middle of the street, over the phone. It wasn't ideal but it had to be done.

From his tiny, wrinkled phone list with the microscopic handwriting, he found her pager number. It was hard to read, since the more numbers he added to the list, the more they bled together. He kept meaning to type this up in the computer lab at school. He paged her "911." Sure it was desperate, but at this point Jeff had to be bold. He didn't want to be banished to the "friend zone" forever.

What was there to lose? Nothing, of course, other than scaring off the love of his life. How long before she called back?

RING!

Not long.

He let it ring a second time, too nervous to pick up. Should he say "Hello?" as if he didn't know who was calling or should he just shout "Katie!" into the receiver? Finally he answered.

"It's Jeff."

"Oh…hey, Jeff. What's up?"

"Sorry to '911' you but I'm at a payphone in Huntington and I needed to talk to you. I was hoping you'd be at the show."

"No, I had plans with my sister."

"Where are you guys? Can I join you?"

Jeff was being pushy. Intrusive. He needed to calm down. He could hear Katie start to ask her sister questions. He couldn't hear the responses.

"Where are we going after this? … Well, where do you want to go? … I don't care …Jeff …Yeah, from the video store."

Frustrated, Jeff quietly murmured to himself, "Just tell me where you are so I can tell you that I love you."

Finally Katie was back on the line. "I'm not sure where we're going next. Oh, shit, the operator needs me to put in more change. Is everything alright? Can we just talk tomorrow?"

No. Jeff had to pull the trigger, right now.

"Look, I know you made out with Nick tonight. And that's fine. You can do whatever you want. But you need to know something. Earlier today I asked Nick for advice. Advice on how to ask you out. Because, Katie, I'm crazy about you. And I told him that. But I also told him I didn't want to rush you. That I wanted to have something meaningful and I knew you just got out of a relationship. He told me to wait before confessing my feelings. That you needed time. And the only reason he did that was so he could make a move on you first. It was a really scummy thing to do. He used us. But it also made me realize that I should have stepped up and told you how I felt. That you're a good friend who wouldn't hold my feelings against me, even if you didn't feel the same way. I was scared to hear you say no. But now I'm not. I don't know how you feel but I'm crazy about you and would love to, well, I'd love to see if we could be more than friends. If that's something you're interested in."

A long pause. Then.

"Um...Jeff, I—"

Click.

The line went dead. He hadn't found out where she was or where she was going. He hadn't gotten a number to call her back. He hadn't been thinking.

What was she going to say?

Um...Jeff, I can't believe you've ruined our friendship? Um...Jeff, I would rather make out with Nick every day for the rest of my life than look at your ugly face again? Um...Jeff, I love you too?

Jeff stood there in stunned silence. Unable to move. What could he do?

160

*****

Jeff's story was fairly typical. So typical that it had no effect on him. He didn't ask for pity. Again, he knew his pain wasn't equal to other people's pain. However, he did know somewhere deep in his subconscious it affected him. That it was one reason he felt so alone.

When Jeff was three years old his mother and father divorced. His father moved off of Long Island to Tenafly, New Jersey, and started a new family, and Jeff pretty much only saw him on Christmas, his birthday and for the occasional ballgame. That was it. They had no real relationship, and this didn't bother Jeff one bit. He was too young when they separated, so there was no actual memory of his parents even being together. Why cry over something you never knew? Sometimes friends would ask why his parents got divorced. The fact is Jeff didn't know and didn't care. It was none of his business. When pressed he'd often suggest the reason was that his father was a diehard Yankees fan and his mother a diehard Mets fan. It was telling that Jeff became a Yankees fan, but he tried not to think about that.

Jeff never had a sibling, or at least one he lived and actually grew up with. So in his early years he played mostly by himself. He'd often run around the living room acting out little stories in his head. He had dozens of imaginary friends to help him in these scenarios. That's all they were, imaginary.

As he got older he started to make more and more real friends. By high school Jeff was considered mildly popular. Friends in all corners of the school. He was very close with many, considering them the brothers and sisters he never had. Others were just friendly acquaintances, but still he felt an odd kinship to them. He liked everybody he met or at least wanted to like them. Jeff didn't judge if they were fat or thin, tall or short, smart or dumb. These people were his real family.

Then why did he feel so constantly lonely?

Jeff could make plans with someone any night of the week, but he wanted more. He wanted someone to share a life with. He wanted to have the kind of love that eluded his parents. And he was terrified he'd never find it. So he invested too much of himself into this journey. And when it inevitably didn't work out....

The counter at the Dix Hills Diner was empty. Since Jeff didn't want to take up a whole booth to himself, he figured just sit there. What was his move? More revenge on Nick? Sic T.J. on him? Or how about drive him way out east, all the way out to Montauk, and abandon him at a payphone by the side of the road. Give him a ton of quarters and tell him to call a friend to pick him up. When no one would be willing to make the two-hour trek to save his butt, he'd realize how little they really cared about him. Despite all the women, all the sex, all the adoring fans, he'd realize how truly alone he was. Would that be considered kidnapping?

No, revenge can wait. First Jeff needed to find out what Katie was going to say. And after all this, he needed it to be that she was willing to take a chance on him. Right now, wherever Katie and her sister were, this had to be the topic of conversation. If it wasn't then Jeff meant nothing to her, even as a friend. Katie was probably so confused. A close confidant was now confessing his feelings. A cool musician was making out with her. A series of weirdos were writing essays to win her love.

"What can I getcha'?" the waitress asked.

"Just coffee."

She started to walk away. Suddenly a lightbulb went off in his head. Jeff knew what he had to do.

"Wait," he said. "Do you have a pen and paper I can borrow?"

"I got a pen, but what kinda paper you want?"

"Like loose-leaf."

"We got receipt paper. I think that's it."

"That works."

Seconds later, laid out in front of Jeff was a fresh cup of coffee, a red pen and a long piece of receipt paper. He had to relent and do what he did best. After all, Jeff was a terrific writer.

Katie,

You now know exactly how I feel about you. There is no reason for me to have to put it in an essay. My original thought was that this is a silly exercise. I stand by that. I have feelings for you and you're either willing to take a chance on me or not.

However, even if I don't think you should need an essay from me, I decided to give you one. Because I want to give you all the things you want. Because I love you.

I don't think I can write this in a traditional essay format, so I guess I am about to lose some points right off the bat. Why you should date me? Here we go:

Because in you I see things I want in my own life. I see ways I would like to be.

Because from the moment I first saw you I thought you were quite possibly the most beautiful woman I ever saw.

Because the first time I saw any of your art I thought you were one of the funniest and most talented people I have ever met.

Because you are beautiful, talented, funny, kind and smart as hell.

Because I feel when I am with you that I can do anything.

Because when I talk about you I cannot help but have a smile on my face.

Because I would do anything if I felt it would benefit your happiness.

Because I will give you what you need, if it be space, if it be anything, just tell me and it's yours.

Because I care about you more than you possibly know.

Because I want to know everything about you. I want to know everyone in your life. I want to be there for everything special that happens for you.

Because I want you to know everything about me, even the embarrassing stuff. I want you to meet everyone I know and be there for me as I accomplish all the things I plan to in this world.

Because I know you and I can be something special.

Because I know the most amazing feeling in the world would be to hold you in my arms. A feeling I know once I've had, I won't be able to live without.

Because I know when I kiss you, the volume will go down on the rest of the world and only you and I will matter.

Because I cannot live in a world where there's a girl I dream about at night and I'm not with her.

Love always...no matter what,

Jeff

There is was. It was pretty heavy but it was from the heart. Scrawled out on a ridiculously long piece of paper was Jeff's last stand for love. Now he just had to deliver it.

T.J.

The events of the day had produced a lot of thoughts on mental health.

In the 1980's many of the one hundred buildings of the massive Kings Park Psychiatric Center had closed down. By the mid-90's the center had been all but abandoned. The problem is, what do you do when you close down a nearly four-hundred-acre psychiatric facility that at one time housed nearly ten thousand patients? Apparently the answer was give them all Thorazine and let them out. The lucky ones would go back home to their families or would be sent to a new hospital. What about the rest?

Kings Park was one town over from Smithtown, and its Psychiatric Center is what it was most known for. Almost immediately after its abandonment, the hospital became the go-to spot for delinquent teens to break into. That's because it was the scariest spot on all of Long Island. Most assumed the area was haunted by the spirits of patients who had died while being given electroshock therapy or lobotomies. There was no actual evidence of ghosts or demons but it sure looked like the kind of place they'd live. The center quickly became run down, overgrown with weeds and vandalized. Most of the old beds and equipment were left to rot within the buildings. The centerpiece of this fright-fest was the massive thirteen-story Building 93, an old brick behemoth with sharp rooftops. From miles away it could be seen creeping above the treetops. The building's height was only matched by its width, as it stretched out like the walls of a fortress. It was rumored that many of the former patients still snuck in there at night and the police had to frequently come round them up.

The entire grounds were dark, lit only by the moon. If you had the guts to break into Building 93, it was pitch black, full of dust and cobwebs and asbestos, and you'd usually have to crawl through a broken window or use a crowbar to pry open a boarded-up door to get in. Between the police, mental patients and a crumbling infrastructure, the place posed real risk. Because of that, this was where T.J. decided to bring Liz next.

As they zipped down the road towards this new adventure, Liz enjoyed her sundae almost as much as she had enjoyed causing frustration to the woman who made it. T.J. still wanted to ask questions about her life. Just as he was trying to figure out a non-awkward way to ask about her love life, she extended her spoon, full of ice cream, fudge, sprinkles, caramel, chocolate chips and all the germs and saliva she carried in her beautiful mouth. T.J. leaned over, struggling to keep his eyes on the road, and gobbled it all up happily.

"I'm going to put something on," Liz said while reaching into her pocket. She pulled out a cassette tape. "Do you like Tom Waits?" she asked.

"I haven't heard a ton of his stuff." T.J. had never heard a single Tom Waits song. He had never even heard the name Tom Waits.

Liz popped the tape in. Out of the car's speakers came a voice that sounded like the love child of whiskey and cigarettes. It was simultaneously alienating and completely inviting. It felt like a story was being told, yet T.J couldn't decipher it. Not in a frustrating way, but in the beautiful way you'll listen to a song over and over again trying to figure out why it makes you feel the way it does.

T.J. stopped himself from reacting to the music with more joy. It was rare he heard something so outside his German industrial wheelhouse and felt this way, but he'd already told a half-lie about pretending to know who Tom Waits was, so he couldn't act too surprised.

"I never heard this one," he said.

"It's great," Liz said. "And at the end this organ comes in and it sounds demonic. Like he's playing an organ in hell. But not in an evil way. Like an organ in hell that's freeing. All the pain in the world is unleashed. You know?"

She was probably misreading the song, but T.J. loved that she thought about it this deeply. He loved that it meant something to Liz. And it made him love her even more.

"In rehab one of my therapists thought I'd be into this," she continued, "and they were right."

The hellish organ she'd mentioned finally came in, just as Building 93 creeped into view. You obviously couldn't park at the Psych Center. The closest spot was a bar a quarter mile away from the grounds. As T.J. searched for parking, a new song clicked on. "Cold Cold Ground."

They listened to the song in silence, really taking it in. Even after they parked, they waited for it to be over before getting out. T.J. couldn't be sure, but he believed this one was about death. Was Liz also thinking about death? Or was it just the specter that hung over this whole day that made him think this. Either way it was beautiful, she was beautiful and maybe life could be beautiful, even knowing it could all be gone in an instant.

*****

Seth had been to the Psych Center enough that he kept the necessary equipment in his trunk. T.J. took the flashlight but opted to leave the crowbar. Last time he and Seth snuck in, they had used the crowbar to rip so-called soothing artwork of ocean views and farmhouses in winter off of the walls. Seth wanted to decorate his room with them, a little reminder he was never too far removed from his own mental breakdown.

T.J. and Liz walked in the moonlight, onto the property and up the hill towards Building 93. Liz was walking hesitantly. T.J. was again in charge.

"If the police see us, we'll have to make a run for it," he explained. "And if there's a crazy mental patient, just stand behind me."

"Have you ever seen a crazy mental patient here? Should we have brought a weapon or something...?"

Other than the graffiti-covered abandoned hospital in front of them, this was actually a fairly romantic setting. An open field. A starry sky. T.J. decided it was time to bring up the subject of dating.

"Do you date a lot at Commack?"

"Are you asking if I'm a slut?"

"No...I..." T.J. stammered.

"I'm just giving you shit. I don't date at all." Liz started to get quieter. "There was this one guy I was kind of seeing for a little while before I went to the clinic. But that ended."

"Was he an asshole? I mean to dump you, he must have been an asshole."

"I don't want to get into it. How about you?"

"I haven't had a girlfriend in…in over a year. That must sound lame."

"Why? I've never really had a boyfriend."

This put T.J. at ease. Maybe he wasn't as big a loser when it came to girls as he thought. He decided to tell her his story.

"I blew it with my ex, Maureen. We dated maybe six months and it was great. We met in photography class. They let you play music in the darkroom while you're developing photos, and she put on Nine Inch Nails and, you know. We'd get high, go to shows and just goof around. Maureen made me feel relaxed, like it was alright to be myself…. So one night we're at a party at Seth's and we go upstairs to fool around. And my friends Jason and Kerri are up there and we walk in while she's giving him head. And he has this legendary massive cock. He knows it so he whips it out whenever he can. Last summer every pool party would turn into him trying to get everyone naked in the pool just to show it off. It's the only thing he's got going for him. It's like his party trick. So we walk in on him getting head and I'd never seen *it* like *that*. And Kerri's embarrassed so we sit around having a big laugh about it. The four of us keep drinking but Jason doesn't put his pants back on. It's weird, right? The whole room smells like sex so we start talking about sex. Maureen and Kerri start talking about blowjobs and Jason starts pushing them into arguing about who gives better head. I thought it was funny, until he gives me a wink and says there's only one way to find out. Suddenly I have a pillow over my face and Maureen and Kerri are both giving me head and it's awesome. I could tell which one was Maureen, she was better anyway, so I declare her the winner. The next thing I know, I'm watching Maureen with Jason's big cock in her mouth. I wanted to throw up. But what could I do? I mean his girlfriend had just gone down on me. He, um, you know, in her mouth and we have a few more drinks but all I want to do is leave. She tried to kiss me later and I couldn't. The next day I broke up with her."

Immediately T.J. regretted telling this story. Hearing it out loud sounded weird and vulgar. He was ashamed he had friends like this. He was ashamed how shitty he had been to Maureen for something they all participated in. Would Liz still want to fuck him? He certainly wouldn't fuck him after hearing something like that. T.J. studied her face. Stone. He stared at her, daring a comment. Finally, out of obligation, she spoke.

"That sucks."

They were now standing directly in front of Building 93.

"There's a way in around the corner," he said. "Come on."

There was a way in, but it still wasn't simple. The door had been knocked over, jammed tightly into the doorway. There was garbage and broken pieces of the building holding it up horizontally, so T.J. and Liz started crawling across the door, slowly. As it wobbled back and forth T.J. would adjust his weight carefully to keep it from collapsing. The dirt the door had acquired over these many months blackened their hands.

"Fuck," a frustrated Liz exclaimed. T.J. turned around and noticed she'd cut her arm on a piece of broken glass, lodged into the doorframe. Blood trickled out of the tear in her sweater.

"Are you alright?" he asked.

Liz didn't respond, she just pushed forward. That's right, she's good with pain.

T.J. climbed off the door and extended a hand to Liz. Dusting themselves off, they took a look down the long medical corridor. This was Building 93. T.J. flipped on the flashlight and led the way.

"This is fucking freaky," Liz said.

"I know. It's almost like something out of *The Broken Movie*."

"Shit, you're right. We need to film something here."

T.J. had been pitching that idea to Jeff for a while but Jeff was too concerned about getting arrested. Besides, Jeff wasn't a horror movie guy. He was more interested in telling stories about teenagers sitting around outside supermarkets, complaining about life.

"Check this out." T.J. shined the light into one of the rooms. At the center was an old hospital gurney, the once-white sheets now a dirty dark grey. There were thick leather straps on either side of it, used to tie down the most troubled patients. Liz's eyes widened with delight. Without a second thought she jumped up on the gurney and lay down as if she was a mental patient.

T.J. walked around, up towards her head. He placed the flashlight under his face, lighting it like a demon.

"Time for your electroshock therapy," he said in his creepiest voice.

He placed the flashlight directly on her right temple and started making a buzzing noise. Liz shook wildly, hurling her body up and down, until finally breaking out in a fit of giggles. T.J. jumped up onto the gurney, putting his arms around her. It was a perfect moment. Should he kiss her? Before he could make his move, she demurred slightly, but still allowed herself to be held in his arms. She looked into his eyes and began to speak slowly and softly.

"In elementary school they made you play an instrument. You had to choose one, but the problem was once you chose it, you were stuck with it for the remainder of your school life. How does a fourth grader know if she'll still want to play the flute when she's a ninth grader? I chose the viola. There were less people playing string instruments, so it felt a little different. And the viola wasn't as typical as a violin and I wouldn't have to lug it around as much as a cello or bass."

T.J. had no idea where this was going. In fact he could barely concentrate on what she was saying. *Kiss her, kiss her, kiss her*.

"I guess I could have been in chorus, but I was too self-conscious to sing. I'm not a good singer. It turns out I'm pretty fucking good at the viola. Good enough that I was the first chair by sophomore year. It's like I didn't even have to practice that much. It came naturally. Weird. But if I sucked at it or if I had chosen the obo or saxophone...."

She paused for a second. Kiss her! T.J. waited too long.

"Mr. Karson was one of the younger teachers. I think it was only his fourth year teaching orchestra. He liked to meet with everyone for private practice after school. Everyone. I didn't think that he thought I was anything special. After, he'd sometimes drive me home or he'd take me for pizza. No one had told me how good I was. Or how pretty I was. And the more time we spent together he'd say things like that. I knew he was married to Mrs. Karson the English teacher but one day during practice I just...kissed him. It was fucking crazy! And he flipped out, telling me that was wrong and he could get fired. I was so embarrassed. But the next week, ugh, I'm so stupid. The next week he still offered to drive me home. And he tells me how he can't stop thinking about the kiss. That he was thinking about me while kissing Mrs. Karson. He said it like he was a victim, like I'd done this to him. And I mean maybe I had, even though I know I didn't really. It's so fucking weird. We were in his car and he just...."

She had paused again. This was it. T.J. put both hands around the sides of her face and pulled her close. He pressed his lips against hers and kissed her hard. She seemed startled. T.J. decided he wasn't going to pull away. Keep kissing her. After what felt like an eternity, Liz slowly parted her lips, kissing him back. Oh my God, this was happening. Taking a chance, he slipped his tongue inside her mouth and began moving it around. She reciprocated.

T.J. began to turn Liz onto her back and carefully climb on top of her. He began grinding his crotch up against hers. This was so much further than he expected he'd be allowed to go. His erection rubbed hard against his underwear and jeans. It hurt just a little, until suddenly he felt free. Liz had unbuttoned his pants and pulled out his penis. This was more than he could have hoped for.

Liz reached into her pocket and pulled out one of her free Planned Parenthood condoms. She quickly slid it onto him. This was all happening so suddenly.

"Are you sure?" T.J. asked.

"Yeah." Her reply didn't sound all that convincing, but before he could overthink it, T.J. was inside of her.

Liz was only the second woman T.J. had ever had sex with. Had being inside Maureen felt different? Better? When T.J. lost his virginity it had been so anticlimactic. Three minutes of squirming around on his then-girlfriend, trying to be quiet and not wake up parents. It wasn't until the third time they had sex that they found a rhythm. That it felt right. He realized there was actually a difference between making love and just fucking. Liz felt good but it would be much better the third, fourth, fifth time they did it.

T.J. was trying really hard not to cum. He wanted this to be a memorable experience for Liz. He looked up at the asbestos-filled ceiling. At the dark, cobweb-filled corners of the room. He tried to concentrate on the squeaking and rattling noises the gurney made. Liz reached behind, grabbing the leather restraints and holding onto them tight. She let out a soft moan and T.J. was about to lose it, until she spoke.

"Call me a slut."

"What?"

"Call me a slut."

He didn't want to call her a slut. He didn't think she was a slut. Do whatever she wants, that was T.J.'s policy.

"Slut," T.J. said apprehensively.

She giggled a little.

"Slut!" This time he said it with more power. He kept saying it over and over. Each time caused her body to shake in an exciting way. But how many times could he call her a slut? He'd have to shake things up.

"Slut! Slut! Slut! *Whore!*"

Liz tensed up, stopping all movement. An annoyed look came across her face.

"I'm a slut. Not a whore."

"I'm sorry," T.J. awkwardly apologized.

"It's alright."

She relaxed again. He continued.

"Slut."

T.J. was close. Try as hard as he might, he couldn't stop himself. He collapsed on top of her. Spent. She wiggled out from under him, quickly. They lay there, breathing heavily. Eventually T.J. pulled the condom off and flung it across the room. It hit the wall with a splat. Yodelayheehoo. How many delinquent kids must have fucked on this gurney?

"I really liked Mr. Karson but I also knew it was wrong. I didn't like what we'd done...so I narced on him. I never saw him again. Fucked up, right?"

T.J. had no idea what she was talking about.

Jackie

When Jackie was fifteen she met a boy. His name was Brandon Bramlet and he went to Sachem High School. Brandon was a senior and Jackie a sophomore. They met at a very early Freaks show, before the band even had a drummer. He was there to see his best friend's punk band Macaroni & Shit.

In between sets, Jackie felt Brandon's eyes on her. He was cute. Messy brown hair and puppy dog eyes, wearing a denim jacket with patches for The Misfits and The Dead Kennedys sewn onto it. A young, wannabe punk. Jackie had hung around punks but never dated one before. So she sent a smile his way, inviting conversation. Brandon had snuck in a flask and the two started to get silly, sneaking sips of some terrible bottom-shelf whisky. Before The Freaks finished their set, Jackie stumbled out with him to his car.

Brandon drove a 1982 Pontiac J-2000. The name J-2000 sounded so futuristic, but the car was a piece of shit. A hand-me-down from a grandmother the family wouldn't let drive anymore. It didn't even have FM radio, so Brandon drove around with a boombox in the front seat from which he blasted all his cassette tapes. Jackie found this both stupid and inventive. It turned out those words could describe Brandon as well. Unlike Jackie, he was terrible student. Straight Ds. What he had were street smarts. You needed a fake ID? Brandon could make a convincing one, no problem. You needed pot last minute? Brandon knew a guy who "owed him." After The Freaks show, they drove in his not-so-futuristic car to an alleyway behind a King Kullen supermarket. At first Jackie was a little nervous to be with some strange, drunk man, in a dark alley. With not much convincing though, Brandon got Jackie into the back seat, her jeans and underwear around her ankles…and proceeded to go down on her.

Eating a girl out was apparently his go-to move. Brandon was good and he knew it. Play to your strengths. This stuck with Jackie. Not because it was the first time in years a high school boy made her cum, but because that's all he wanted to do. Of course guys would go down on her, but only as a form of reciprocation. They felt obligated. Brandon first and foremost wanted to make a woman feel special. He was chivalrous, and it charmed her, until of course it didn't.

Jackie and Brandon dated for four months. At that time it was Jackie's longest relationship, and she was beginning to feel stifled. She liked Brandon a lot but wanted to try being with other boys, have different experiences. Brandon was a senior, so he'd gotten girls and sex out of his system. Jackie was only a sophomore and still needed to be free to try new things. New people. Even at the time Jackie worried her reasons for breaking Brandon's heart sucked, but they were real and honest. She broke the news to him real and honest. Brandon did not take it well.

Jackie debated lying, telling him her mom was putting pressure on her to stop dating such a delinquent. That her grades had been slipping. Some bullshit like that. Instead she explained she was too young to be in a monogamous relationship right now. Brandon was confused. He couldn't understand why he wasn't enough for her. Why what they had wasn't enough. Brandon, who'd never done a cruel thing to her in their relationship, called her a slut. A whore. A cum dumpster. Jackie decided not to hold it against him. It was the heat of the moment. In a day or two he'd probably call or show up after school to apologize. He'd probably even try and win her back. Instead, a day or two later, Brandon did something unthinkable.

The call came just as Jackie was making her way to the bus stop. It was from the vice principal. Jackie's mother hung up the phone, raced outside and grabbed her before she had even reached the end of the driveway. Apparently there'd been a prank and Jackie was the victim. Her mother explained this to her. Something involving spray paint. Jackie's mom wasn't the best at relaying information and the fact she was so emotional made it even harder for Jackie to understand. So what? There was a prank. How bad could it be? Apparently bad enough for the police and a school counselor to be on their way over. They wanted to ask Jackie if she had any enemies. Brandon.

Whatever happened Jackie wanted to see it for herself. Brandon probably just spray painted "Jackie sux dick" in the parking lot or some stupid shit. They were probably overreacting. If she waited until tomorrow the prank would already be cleaned up. Whatever had happened, it was about her and she needed to know. Needed to know how big a jerk Brandon was and what the blowback at school might be. It was her right. Besides, she wanted to show the school that no one could bully her. Before the police arrived, while her mother was on the phone awkwardly explaining why she couldn't go in to work, Jackie snuck out.

She hadn't ridden a bike in at least two years, and yes, you can forget. So Jackie awkwardly rode as fast as she could up to the high school. By now she knew her mother would have figured out where she was going. Mom was sure to be out looking for her, so Jackie stuck to the side roads.

Finally she made it up to the high school. Jackie was right, Brandon had spray painted the parking lot. And the school's sign. And the doors of the front entrance. And the sides of the building. All the windows. The bleachers. The tennis courts. The track. Even a school bus that had been left in the parking lot overnight.

Brandon had spray painted one hundred and twenty-three times, one time for every day they dated, a certain phrase across Smithtown High School property.

JACKIE SPAM HAS AIDS

This was bad. Every single student would see this, and all of them, even if they didn't really believe she had AIDS, would think she was a slut. Hell, the students who didn't know her already felt that way. It would always be remembered that Jackie Spampinato had AIDS.

Looking out over the school and seeing in bright red paint these words, Jackie made an important decision. She wouldn't be embarrassed by this. Instead she would get mad. She would lean into her reputation. Jackie wouldn't be shamed into being some chaste little girl. Fuck these people. Fuck them all. This wasn't always an easy attitude to have, and sometimes in moments of weakness she'd be filled with doubt or catch herself crying. Despite that, Jackie remained determined to be her flawed, convoluted self, and if people didn't like it, then she didn't like them.

Two years later Jackie was in the back seat of a virtual stranger's car. A stranger who probably knew her best as the girl who has AIDS. Marie and Adam were bringing her to Sage's party.

Adam drove, while Marie, sitting shotgun, lit a cigarette already dangling from her lips. She took a puff or two before looking back at Jackie in the back seat. Jackie stared out the window, her mind clearly lost in another world.

"Smoke?" Marie asked, offering her the cigarette.

Jackie took it from Marie's hand. Can you get hepatitis from sharing a cigarette? Probably not. Fuck it. She took a slow, long drag.

"You were badass," Marie offered. Jackie already knew she was badass.

BEEP BEEP BEEP

943

It was coming from Sage, or at least Sage's house. Maybe it was Jeff waiting to shit on her boyfriend. Unbeknownst to him, Jackie had already taken care of that.

*****

Whenever given the opportunity, Sage loved to throw a party. They'd always start off with the intention of a small gathering. Oh, my parents are going out of town for a few days, why don't three or four of you come by, we'll get drunk and watch movies. Inevitably "three or four of you" would turn into thirty or forty of you. Because Sage loved parties. And tonight she might have outdone herself.

There were not "three or four" party guests. There were not "thirty or forty." There were easily a hundred fifty, and that might be a low estimate. Jackie knew the party was out of control when Marie had trouble finding a parking spot. Sage lived in Nissequogue, a four-square-mile village that was part of Smithtown. Nissequogue was also the richest part of town. It bordered the Long Island Sound and its streets were mostly narrow dirt roads. There were no streetlights, because such things might ruin the beauty of the night sky, a beauty only the rich, like Sage's parents, could afford. Sage's house was the largest of anyone

Jackie personally knew, and tonight it had teenagers of every stripe pouring in and out of it. In a neighborhood like this, it was only a matter of time before someone called the cops.

They entered the house, pushing past drunken teens milling about on the front lawn. Marie and Adam headed towards the back yard, in search of booze, while Jackie marched into the living room. She was on a mission to find Jeff or anyone she was close to. Jackie pushed past dozens of partygoers and had not recognized a single person. Who were all these people?

Standing on top of a coffee table in the living room was Sage. She wore a babydoll dress and was dancing in an ethereal manner. Sage did not have the kind of looks that would stop traffic. She was a beautiful girl, no doubt, but what made her one of the most desired girls at Smithtown High was that she was truly comfortable in her own skin. There was not one false note about her. Jackie remembered Sage being this way from when she was a freshman. Even now, Jackie remained impressed with the way Sage stayed true to herself, something most seniors couldn't even do without risk of embarrassment. Jackie stared, taking her in. The hip hop beats that blared from the stereo were The Beastie Boys' "So What'cha Want," and yet Sage's slow, dreamlike dancing could only be coming from music playing inside her own head. There was no shame about this. Sage wanted to dance the way Sage wanted to dance. An adult might see her and assume she was on drugs. But Sage never did drugs. This was Sage's drug. Being surrounded by revelers, having themselves a hedonistic good time. She got off on this.

"Jackie!" Sage's eyes lit up as she jumped down from the table and ran over to hug her friend. She threw both arms around Jackie. Jackie needed this embrace.

"Who are all these people?" Jackie asked.

"Beats me," Sage replied. "I passed out a few flyers after school. And then I went over to Commack and handed out some flyers there. And Kings Park."

"You passed out flyers at three different schools?"

"Oh, Hauppauge too! You know, I was going to have a small get-together, just three or four people. But the whole Nirvana thing had so many people down, I wanted to give everyone a way to get their minds off it."

Sage beamed a huge smile Jackie's way. Always thinking of others.

"Hey," Sage continued, "where's this man of yours?"

Fuck. Jackie knew she'd eventually ask, but somehow hoped with the craziness of the party she'd forget.

"He couldn't make it. Some big...college...exam...thing...." Jackie stammered through this response in a way that clearly showed she was lying. Making a bad excuse for a man she wasn't even dating anymore. Luckily, she wasn't talking to Jeff. Sage was a free spirit who always wanted to believe you. She always took everyone at their word.

"Oh, that sucks. I was hoping to meet him."

Why was Jackie lying? By morning everyone would know the truth. Marie was probably telling people right now about the Dix Hills Diner incident.

Sage grabbed Jackie's hand and started dragging her towards the kitchen. They pushed past stoners, drunks and a couple that was making out in the doorway.

"Did you beep me?" Jackie asked.

183

"No."

"Is Jeff here?"

"I don't know, there's a lot of people so...*maybe*? Let's get you a drink!" As they finally pushed into the kitchen Jackie saw a sight she hadn't expected. Mountains of Tupperware, all filled with bright red cherry Jell-O.

Sage started looking around. "Let's see, we have whiskey and vodka over there. Soda in the fridge if you want to mix something. *Someone* brought a keg, it's in the back yard."

Jackie didn't hear a word Sage was saying. She just kept looking at the Jell-O. There were stacks of it on the kitchen table, the counters, even on top of the refrigerator. As she was trying to make sense of all this, some jock in a football jersey popped open one of the containers, stuck his hand in, grabbing a fistful of sticky gelatin. The usually laid-back Sage blew a fuse.

"Hey, that's not for eating! Get away!" She marched over to him and ripped the Tupperware out of his hands. The confused jock wandered off.

"Jell-O shots?" Jackie asked.

"I asked everyone to make cherry Jell-O and bring it over because I wanted to submerge myself in it. I'm worried we don't have enough."

Jackie glanced at all the containers again. It seemed like more than enough to cover Sage's body.

"The plan," Sage continued, "was to drain all the water from the swimming pool and replace it with Jell-O."

"You want to swim in it?" Jackie asked.

184

"It's my dream. Just imagine how it'd feel to sink your whole body into a pool of Jell-O. It'd feel so soft to float on. Like a waterbed but better. And you know that sound and feeling when you break the surface of Jell-O with a spoon? Imagine if your body was the spoon! I thought if we had enough Jell-O to fill the pool, I could float on it during the party. Eventually I'd have to let other people dive in. I assume T.J. would end up ruining things by jerking off in it. But I'd go first and it'd be glorious."

This was the stupidest dream Jackie had ever heard. And she loved Sage for it. The sheer whimsical idiocy would have made Sean angry, and for that reason alone, it was too bad he wasn't here.

*****

Jackie had been at the party for a good half hour and hadn't seen anyone she cared to talk to. She wandered the large back yard, slowly drinking a beer. Rather than get a cup of swill from the keg, she had found a Heineken in the fridge. On one side of the yard, a slew of metalheads were slam-dancing to some industrial music she didn't recognize. On the other, Marie sat on lawn furniture, holding court. No doubt she was talking about Jackie.

Jackie stood over the pool, looking down into the water. There seemed to be a large object at the bottom of the deep end.

"Is that a barbeque?" a voice asked from behind her. She turned around to see Nick LeWinter, smoking a cigarette and staring at the pool.

"I think so," Jackie said.

"They threw her barbeque into the pool? Animals. Why's the pool even opened?" Nick questioned.

"Sage wanted to fill it with Jell-O."

"That explains a lot."

Nick offered her a cigarette. She accepted. They began wandering away from the party together. Deeper into the back yard.

"Where's your boyfriend?" Nick asked.

Jackie took a long drag, contemplating lying again.

"I dumped him."

"Really? Why?"

"Because he didn't believe in dinosaurs."

Nick didn't question this, and there was good reason why. Now that she was single, Nick was going to try and fuck her. Jackie couldn't blame him. It's just what Nick did.

"Have you seen Jeff? I think he beeped me from here," she said.

"I beeped you," Nick said.

"Why?"

"Things seemed weird at the show. I put you in an awkward spot so I was hoping you'd be here. Wanted to clear the air."

"About the fact I used to date another guy named Sean?" Jackie questioned.

"He seemed bothered by it. I didn't cause you guys to break up?"

Nick didn't give a shit whether he caused her breakup or not. In fact, he'd be happy if he had. Had he actually tried to make Sean jealous on purpose? The page Nick sent wasn't out of concern. It was some weird way to lay the groundwork for his next move. This is what Nick does. Screws with your relationship. He wants to fuck everyone's girlfriend. He wants to piss off everyone's boyfriend.

"I told you," Jackie said with authority. "He didn't believe in dinosaurs. So I ended it."

Nick put his hands in the air as if to say "o.k., I get it." The pair had wandered as far away from the party as they could without leaving Sage's property. They gazed out at the hundred or so kids. Through the windows they could see all three stories of the house were jam-packed.

There was an old shed that Nick leaned up against. He scraped the butt of his cigarette against the door, extinguishing it, before dropping it in the grass. Jackie did the same. Then he slowly opened the shed, taking a step inside. Jackie just stared at him, realizing they had walked over here to this out-of-the-way place on purpose. Nick made a motion with his head, telling Jackie to come inside. She didn't give it a second thought.

The shed was a typical shed. Cobwebs, dirty, filled with lawn tools. How many girls had Nick brought here? He closed the door behind them, then pushed Jackie up against it, hard, and began to kiss her. The action was so sudden, Jackie dropped what was left of her Heineken on the floor. Then she reciprocated.

It had been at least a year since she'd last kissed Nick. She'd forgotten one of the reasons he got laid all the time was that he was a pretty great kisser. The kissing quickly evolved to groping and groping evolved to Nick unbuttoning his pants. Jackie stopped him.

"Do you have a condom?" she asked.

"It's alright. I know you don't have AIDS."

"But I don't know you don't."

Nick stepped back, frustrated. He slowly slumped to the ground. Jackie sat down next to him. He placed his head on her shoulder and they sat in silence.

After a few minutes of quiet, Nick was at it again. He began softly kissing her neck and Jackie couldn't help but let out a soft moan. She looked down. His pants were still unbuttoned and now he had taken his dick out. Fully erect.

"Please..." he begged.

Nick was acting pathetic. Begging for it was beneath him. She reached down and slowly started to jerk him off. His head kicked back, hitting the shed wall, as he moaned. Nick didn't want a handjob but he'd settle for one. No guy *really* wants a handjob. It's the consolation prize of sexual acts. Tonight, though, it was all Jackie was willing to give.

Jackie wasn't sure how much time had passed, but this was taking forever. Her wrist was getting tired and the skin on his penis was starting to feel raw. Five minutes? Ten? Time stood still in the shed. For a moment Jackie considered going down on him, just to get this over with. Then, suddenly, Nick let out a whimper. It was over.

"Fuck. What a mess," he said.

There was a dirty rag over on the workbench. Jackie grabbed it, handing it to him. Nick cleaned himself up.

"Go down on me," Jackie suddenly declared.

"What?"

"You heard me. Go down on me right now."

Nick scoffed.

"I'm not joking," she continued.

Nick gave her a sly smile. "You didn't go down on me."

He proceeded to slide his hand along her inner thigh and up her skirt. Then he creeped two of his fingers past her underwear, inside her.

Jackie closed her eyes. She needed this. She'd rather it had been with someone other than Nick, but it still felt good. Jackie and Nick were the same. Two nonjudgmental people who used sex for pleasure. The only difference being that Nick was admired by every man she knew while Jackie was a pariah for it.

Her body began to shake. She was close. Opening her eyes Jackie looked up at the ceiling. Her shaking was causing the shed to shake, which caused the tools hanging above to shake. Hedge clippers. Hoes. Sharp-edged tools, violently shifting back and forth, looking like they could fall at any moment. Jackie imagined them crashing down upon them. Impaling and killing Nick. At that moment she climaxed.

*****

Jackie stood over a bowl of potato chips, scarfing them down. Recent activities had made her hungry again. It'd feel so much better to be at home, alone in bed, watching a movie with a big bowl of popcorn. Somehow more and more people had flooded into the party, and yet Jackie knew none of them. Sage was still dancing to the music in her head. Marie was still gossiping. Adam still looking at Marie like a lost puppy. And Nick was now hanging with a group of guys she didn't know but suspected were from the music scene. All while Jackie ate chip after chip. She'd become this party's ultimate voyeur. Taking it all in. No one was noticing her. It was as if she didn't exist.

Nick and the boys were snickering. Then he held up two fingers. The two fingers that just twenty minutes ago had been inside her. She watched as Nick shoved them under some spiky haired loser's nose. Spiky recoiled in disgust, laughing. Jackie could have sworn she saw him mouth the word "fish."

No matter what she did or who she did it with, Jackie just couldn't win. She marched over to Marie, interrupting her story.

"I gotta get out of here." Jackie's voice was quivering with desperation.

Marie put down her drink and stood up. Adam mirrored this motion.

"O.k., we can go."

Marie said this in a condescending tone that annoyed Jackie. She'd already been made to feel like a child today. At the same time, it was a nice gesture. A human gesture. Marie was willing to leave a party where everyone was having a good time. Everyone but Jackie. Jackie must have looked pretty desperate to elicit such kindness.

"My car is in Stony Brook. Can you take me there?"

Marie looked at Adam. He was on it. Within seconds the three of them were leaving.

Matt

Matt was now singing and loudly humming along to the radio. He continued to complain about how he'd been treated, with no response from Tariq other than turning on the radio. At first this move seemed to be made simply to shut Matt up. But Matt decided Tariq was just trying to calm him down the only way he knew how. And it worked. Matt was feeling much calmer. And now a song he loved was playing. So why not embrace it. Change up the mood. Sing along to break the silence.

He wasn't going to pretend to know more about the Crash Test Dummies beyond this one song; after all, they weren't Nirvana. Matt did legitimately like the song. It told a clear story that he understood. Children suffering in isolation. Not that Matt knew suffering like that. Mulatto, albino, those were just a bunch of words. This was a story.

Tariq was not singing along. Was it because he didn't like the song or just didn't know the lyrics? Then again nothing about Tariq screamed that he was the sing-along type. Instead he just continued to munch on his Twizzlers, speeding down Route 347 towards the Commack Blockbuster.

As *"Mmm Mmm Mmm Mmm"* wound down, Matt stayed with it until every last "*oh*" was finished. He was back to his usual self and ready for conversation.

"Before the middle schools merged, you went to Accompsett, right?" Matt asked.

"Yeah."

"You know, before Nesaquake closed they decided to make a yearbook celebrating our brief time there. And they decided to take a poll on things like what the students' favorite TV shows or movies were. Everyone had pretty similar answers. Where there was a huge divide was on music. Every boy was voting for Guns N' Roses and every girl was voting for New Kids on the Block. The boys fought hard to make sure everyone voted for Guns N' Roses. We didn't want those New Kids pussies to be in our yearbook. So on the last day of school, we got our yearbooks and immediately flipped to the back page where the results were. And the New Kids won! I couldn't believe that for all of time the 1989 class's favorite band would be New Kids on the Block. Now here's the crazy part. There were more boys in the class than girls. By a considerable number, too. So what the hell happened? I always suspected the school rigged it. They didn't want a band like Guns N' Roses to be represented in the yearbook. Or maybe the administration just didn't want the word 'gun' in the yearbook. It pissed me off. It still does. I wasn't even a huge Guns N' Roses fan, but it just wasn't fair."

No one said anything for a few seconds. Why had Matt suddenly had this memory? Finally Tariq responded.

"Maybe they were lying."

"Who was lying?" Matt questioned.

"The boys. Maybe they didn't vote for Guns N' Roses."

"No. We were all together on this one."

"Maybe some boys really liked New Kids on the Block," Tariq speculated.

"I seriously doubt that," Matt said with the utmost confidence.

"You don't know. It's a more reasonable theory than some administration conspiracy."

"Why lie?"

"Because they didn't want to be 'pussies' for liking the New Kids," Tariq said.

In all these years, this idea had never once occurred to Matt.

"I get why you *think* that might be the case, but I'm telling you, I lived this. I'd buy that *maybe* there was a group of boys that really liked Metallica or something and voted for them instead, but then why lie about it?" Matt asked.

"Some people like to lie."

*****

Matt stormed into the second Blockbuster like a man possessed. It was somewhat typical for them to be going to multiple Blockbusters in one night, but this felt different. He had blown the idea of finding *Over the Edge* way out of proportion and he knew it. Matt just wanted a win. He felt he deserved one.

Tariq followed a few feet behind.

"I'm going to check the sections," Matt shouted back to him. "Why don't you ask up front?"

Drama. **O**. *The Outsiders*. *Paper Moon*. Fuck.

Action. **O**. *Over the Top*. Fuck.

Matt struggled to think if there was a third section he should check. It didn't sound like a comedy, but clearly some of these Blockbuster employees didn't know what the hell they were doing.

Slowly he walked the aisles, heading towards the front of the store where hopefully Tariq was having better luck.

The Commack Blockbuster was very close to where Rebecca lived. Suddenly this fact preoccupied Matt. He'd probably never speak to her again, and with every passing minute he seemed more and more comfortable with that fact.

Matt was willing to take a chance on any girl, but of the few he went out on actual real live dates with, he always found flaws that prevented him from wanting to take things further. He knew this about himself but couldn't do anything to stop it. Jeff more than anyone else had sympathy for Matt's disastrous love life. He'd try to help him by setting Matt up with friends from other schools. Matt assumed most of these girls had previously dated or rejected Jeff. This didn't bother him. He wasn't above sloppy seconds. These women, however, were such disasters, Matt started to question what Jeff's actual opinion of him was. Did Jeff really think these were the kind of women worthy of him?

Take Amy, a girl Jeff knew from his camp days. Back in the brief period when Jeff and Jackie dated they invited Matt out, along with Amy, for a double date. Jeff and Jackie had really built Amy up. They told Matt she was sweet and cute. They also admitted she was on the quiet side but figured since Matt was a talker, he could carry all the conversation. Amy was sweet. Amy was cute. Amy was also a fucking idiot. After dinner at the Millennium the four of them went to a playground to hang out and goof around on slides and seesaws, like when they were kids. Playgrounds at night are a quiet, peaceful place to talk and make out. Jeff and Jackie disappeared for some time, leaving Matt and Amy alone on the swings, gazing up at the stars. It was a romantic moment, and Matt wondered if he should try and kiss this sweet, cute girl. His first kiss. Instead, while looking up at the night sky,

Matt made an offhand comment. "In space no one can hear you scream." Amy didn't recognize it as the famous tagline to the film *Alien*. When Matt explained it, Amy questioned the logic. "If you make a noise you make a noise, someone can hear it." Matt spent the next half hour trying to teach her about how sound cannot travel through the vacuum of space. She kept insisting that if you scream you scream and it makes a sound. She felt it was a stupid tagline. Ridiculous.

Or there was that time Jeff played wingman at a Freaks show and introduced Matt to a sexy emo girl in a tight turtleneck sweater. After an hour of conversation that seemed to be going well, she mentioned how she hated *Star Wars*. *Star Wars*, only the alpha and omega of their generation's popular culture. How could anyone not like it? Matt pressed her on this issue, demanding a reason. She couldn't quite explain it. She just didn't like it. This really pissed Matt off. It's one thing to not like something, it's another thing to not be able to explain why. There was obviously a reason she didn't like the greatest film franchise of all time, but you have to communicate it. Sexy emo girl clearly lacked some basic mental skills. How could they ever have a real conversation?

As Matt approached the counter he saw that Tariq was in conversation with the female clerk. No, not just conversation, they were laughing. She had short black hair and a septum ring. Her nametag read "Alison."

"I love her so much. In fact, I've been thinking of dying my hair red," Alison said, a huge smile across her face.

"That'd be awesome," Tariq replied.

Matt approached, desperately wanting to know what was going on. Before he could say anything, Alison pointed at Matt's *X-Files* shirt and shouted "Scully!" She and Tariq laughed.

"What?" Matt shouted back.

"Mulder," Alison said, pointing to Tariq. "Scully," she then said, pointing back at Matt.

"Yeah," Matt said annoyed. "He didn't tell me he was wearing that shirt today."

"Alison is a huge *X-Files* fan," Tariq said.

"Dana Scully is my hero!" she exclaimed.

How long had Matt been wandering the aisles? Long enough for Tariq and this Alison girl to become best friends.

"I love your guys' shirts. I have a big 'I Want To Believe' poster in my room. I usually make sure I'm off Fridays so I can watch, but luckily tonight's a rerun."

"What's your favorite episode?" Tariq asked.

"'Beyond the Sea.' It's a great Scully one."

The t-shirt. Yes, that's what started the conversation. Damn. If only Matt had gone to the counter, he'd be alone with her. He'd have a chance to flirt. Alison certainly had a cute-enough face. Matt tried to take the rest of her in. It was hard to tell since she was behind the counter, but her body seemed pear-shaped. She was thin on top but her hips and ass looked pretty big. Matt could live with that. It actually made her more attainable. If only Tariq would shut up for a second and let him into the conversation.

"My favorite is 'Ice,'" Tariq said. "I love when—"

Matt decided to interrupt.

"I have all the episodes on tape. We watch them every weekend. You should tape them. It's better anyway, you can fast-forward through the commercials."

Alison gave Matt a slight smile and turned back to Tariq. Fast-forward through commercials? She knows what a VCR does. Idiot. Matt was losing her.

"Hey, so what's the deal with *Over the Edge*?" Matt asked.

Alison and Tariq seemed distracted, looking at each other. It took her a second to snap out of it and answer.

"Oh. That movie's out of print," she said.

"Out of print? How do you know?" Matt questioned.

"It says in the computer." She turned her attention back to Tariq, but Matt wasn't finished.

"Would it say that in the computers at all Blockbusters?"

"Of course," Alison answered.

Matt got angry again. "Then why would that retard in Hauppauge not say that!"

"I...I don't know." Again she tried to turn to Tariq. Again Matt was relentless.

"Can you order it?"

"No," Alison said in a clipped tone. "It's out of print. They don't make it anymore."

Matt realized if he was going to have any chance with this girl he'd have to calm down.

"You know it was Kurt Cobain's favorite movie. We wanted to watch it tonight as sort of a tribute to him. Crazy about Kurt, right?"

Holy shit. Matt couldn't believe what he just saw. Tariq rolled his eyes, right in Alison's direction. It was blatant, as if to say about Matt, "Can you believe this idiot?" What kind of friend was he? It was time to go.

"Hey Tariq, maybe 112 Video has it. They have all sorts of out-of-print stuff."

"That's like, an hour away," Tariq said.

"No. It's like forty minutes. Let's go before they close."

Matt was trying to rush Tariq out the door, but he was following slowly, as if he didn't want to leave.

"Come on," Matt demanded. "Let's go."

Tariq smiled a sad smile at Alison and quietly headed out the door. Then in his flirtiest voice Matt said "Alison, thank you for your help. You are wonderful. I will come to you for all my video needs."

Alison forced a smile and watched as the boys walked into the parking lot.

*****

"Can you believe it? Out of print. Why didn't the first guy tell us that? What a waste of a night," Matt ranted.

Tariq's car sped down the dark Nesconset Highway. He was driving faster than Matt had ever recalled. Tariq's hands gripped the steering wheel tight, his face dead serious.

"I want to rent this movie too, but you're going kind of fast there, buddy."

Tariq slammed on the brakes. Matt was propelled forward, then thrown back by the seatbelt. All the garbage in the car shifted. Some old soda cans and candy wrappers flew from the back seat into the front. Matt's jaw dropped. He was speechless. Tariq was breathing heavily, like some crazed animal.

"Is Rebecca real?" Tariq asked.

"What?" Matt was confused by the question.

"Is Rebecca real? Are you really dating and not fucking a girl named Rebecca?" Tariq was angry. Matt suddenly found himself on the defensive.

"Of course, she's real. What do you think I am? Some sort of psycho?"

"Then why were you flirting with Alison?"

"Because…I told you it's not going to work with Rebecca. I'm not married." Matt let out a flippant laugh. He didn't understand what the big deal was.

"Why did you cock-block me?" Tariq demanded to know.

"When did I cock-block you?"

"*I* was flirting with Alison. *I* was hitting on her. And then you came in and messed up my shit."

Oh. That's what the big deal was. In the three years he had known Tariq he'd never heard him talk about girls. He never saw him ask a girl out. Matt viewed him as a non-sexual being.

"I didn't know," Matt said. "I didn't realize she was your type."

"A cute weirdo who loves *The X-Files* wouldn't be my type?!?"

"You never talk about girls so—"

"Because you never shut up! You never shut up and ask me about them! You never ask me who I'm interested in. And supposedly you have this gorgeous girlfriend from Dix Hills, but no one's ever seen her. It smells like your typical bullshit."

"Wait, Tariq, I'm—"

"If Rebecca was real, if this beautiful Jewish princess were real, why are you pushing me out of the way to hit on a girl at Blockbuster? Why aren't you home fucking her? Was she even sick or is she totally made up? You know, I was really looking forward to you losing your virginity tonight, not because I was happy for you, but so I don't have to hear about it anymore! I'm a virgin. Do I go on about it? And then you call me up and send us on this wild goose chase looking for a movie that probably sucks, as what, some way to honor a musician you never even listened to! I wanted to go to Sage's party. Instead I have to drive around listening to you complain about my t-shirt and steal my first celebrity crush. Your first celebrity crush wasn't Winona in *Beetlejuice*. That was mine! I always called her dark and weird in an approachable way. Your first celebrity crush was Madonna in the 'Like a Virgin' video. You've said that a thousand times. But you have to have everything. You have to be the center of attention. Everything with you is a tragedy we all have to care about. I'm fucking sick of it!"

This was easily the most Tariq had ever spoken at one time. Matt was floored. He couldn't be angry, though. Tariq was right. Especially about cock-blocking him. Instead Matt felt deep embarrassment. He started to open his mouth, trying to say sorry, but no words came out.

"Get out of the car," Tariq said.

"Out here? How will I get home?" Matt's embarrassment was turning to panic. Would Tariq really abandon him on the side of a dark highway?

"Please get out." Tariq said this so calmly it freaked Matt out. Tariq was resigned to end this friendship, right here on Nesconset Highway. Slowly Matt opened the door and stepped outside.

"What are you going to do?" Matt asked.

"Go to Sage's. Or maybe I'll go back and get Alison's number."

Matt closed the door and Tariq drove off into the night.

He was all alone.

Jeff

Despite all the time Jeff and Katie had spent together these last few months, he had no clue where she lived. They would always hang out after work or at a show. Or they'd meet up at a diner. Jeff had an idea about someone who might know more. A guy who had driven her home one night after a show. And he was pretty sure this guy would be in the same place he always was.

The King Kullen parking lot was empty except for the skateboarders. Zack and Eric Hodrinsky, along with Zack's longtime girlfriend Jane, stood around their Camry, staring at a goldfish in a plastic bag. On the hood of their car was a sleeve of saltine crackers. Why did people have trouble telling the Hodrinskys apart? Yes, they were identical twins who dressed similarly, and both had shaved heads, but Eric had a slightly longer face and Zack a bigger nose. Why was this confusing?

Jeff distinctly remembered one night after a Freaks show watching Katie climb into the back of that rusty old Camry. It was before they'd become close and he regretted not offering her a ride home himself. It didn't matter, she had a boyfriend. Still, any lost moment with Katie was something to mourn. That night Eric drove her home. The same Hodrinsky who Jeff last saw furiously writing an essay to Katie in the mall food court. If Jeff wanted to hand in his assignment to Katie tonight, Eric was his best hope. The question was, would this fellow suitor be willing to help the competition?

"Hey Eric, Zack, Jane, what's with the fish?" Jeff figured start off with some small talk before building to the big request. Also, what *was* with the fish? Wait, what was with the saltine crackers?

"I won it at a carnival in Islip!" Jane said. "I'm thinking of naming him Blinky."

"I wouldn't get too attached. Those fish don't have a long lifespan," Jeff reminded her.

Jane gave Jeff a dirty look before her attention returned to Blinky. "Don't listen to him," she said to the fish. Jeff and the Hodrinskys gave each other knowing glances. They knew this poor fish wasn't long for the world.

"You know," Eric started, "there are these poor fucking people who smell like fish. It's a disease or some shit. Imagine going through life like that?"

Oh no. There's only one person who could have told Eric this.

"I've heard of that before," Jeff replied. "Some long, unpronounceable word."

"Fuck that," Zack said with a laugh. "I'd rather eat a shotgun than go through life stinking like a fish."

Jane slapped Zack upside the head, which only caused him to laugh more. Jeff once again had completely forgotten about Kurt.

"Hey, have any of you guys seen Katie tonight?" Jeff asked.

"I saw her at Hot Topic, but that was hours ago," Eric answered.

"I have something for her and was hoping to get it to her tonight. I tried calling but I keep getting the machine. Do you know where she lives? I figured if she's still out I can leave it at the door."

Eric gave Jeff a knowing smile.

"You're in the essay contest."

"…Yeah."

"What essay contest?" Jane asked.

"It's embarrassing," Jeff started. He didn't want to say any more because it was embarrassing. Being made to compete with a bunch of dudes to win a girl's heart. It was like the stupidest episode of *Love Connection*. Jeff had thought he was better than this, but clearly, he wasn't. Eric would explain it, allowing Jeff to at least preserve a little bit of dignity.

"Katie, that weird, hot chick who sells buttons at shows, she's single again. And I guess a lot of guys started hitting on her all at once. So she decided to have an essay contest to see which one she'd date. I gave her mine this afternoon."

"That's gross!" Jane objected. All three boys were taken aback by her burst of outrage. "Who does this bitch think she is that she's got all these guys writing essays about wanting to be with her? What an ego. She's not all that. Stop giving this chick attention."

"Whatever," Eric said dismissively.

Jeff knew Jane was right. What was this for Katie if not an ego trip? Why was Jeff playing into this by actually writing the essay? Because he knew if she did choose him, it wouldn't be because he fed her ego the best. It would be because she saw how much he loved her. After all, he was asked to help judge the essays. Wasn't he in on the joke?

"So, Eric," Jeff began delicately. "I know you drove her home once. I was wondering if you could tell me where she lives."

Eric started to open his mouth when Zack cut him off. "Don't tell this fucker where she lives. Don't *you* want to win the contest?"

Eric stopped, clearly thinking it over.

"Come on," Jeff pleaded. "If you don't tell me I'm just going to bring it to her tomorrow."

"Why don't you just bring it to her tomorrow?" Eric asked.

"I'd rather do it tonight. It's been a bad day. I want to at least end it with a small victory." Jeff said this with sincerity. He really believed time was of the essence. Whether or not this was true no longer mattered.

"I'll tell you what," Eric said. "I'll tell you where she lives if you can beat the saltine cracker challenge."

"And what's the saltine cracker challenge?" Jeff asked.

"You have to eat six saltine crackers in sixty seconds."

"That doesn't sound hard," Jeff said, with an air of superiority in his voice.

"No one can do it," Jane said. "Zack thought he could, but he barely got three down."

"Four!" Zack protested.

How hard could this be? All Jeff had to do was eat six crackers in less than a minute and he'd get Katie's address. It wouldn't be the dumbest or most difficult thing he'd done for love tonight.

"Give me the crackers."

Eric removed six saltines from the sleeve and handed them to Jeff.

"Tell me when," Jeff said.

Eric took what felt like an eternity to say when, as he waited for a new minute to start on his cheap cereal-box wristwatch.

"Go!"

Jeff had two choices. Shove all six crackers in his mouth at once or do one at a time. In went all six! The sooner they were all in his mouth, the sooner they'd be down this throat. This decision produced an audible gasp from Jane and a bit of giggling from the Hodrinskys.

Jeff chewed and chewed and chewed but he was hardly able to swallow a thing. He could feel the mushy crackers building up in his cheeks. He looked ridiculous. Like a chipmunk. How much time had passed? All the saliva in his mouth was gone, soaked up by the dry crackers. He managed to get a little bit down. Then a little more. And a little more. He had to keep swallowing. Swallowing for Katie.

"Time!"

That was fast. Jeff still had half the crackers in his mouth. It was impossible. Defeated, he spit what was left out onto the ground, to the delight of his audience. The night would end in its usual sad fashion after all.

"I got about half. Will you give me directions halfway to her place?" Jeff half joked.

Eric smiled. "I'll tell you where she lives."

"Fuck that," his brother chimed in.

"I don't care," Eric said. "She's not gonna date me anyway. My essay sucked."

Jeff tried to hold in his excitement. Play it cool.

"Go past the lake, towards Ronkonkoma, then turn left, right before the movie theater. She's, I think the third right, or was it the fourth, one of those. But you can't miss her house. It has a white picket fence. The American dream, ya know?"

*****

Twenty-three minutes later Jeff was standing in front of the American dream.

Katie must have still been out, since he didn't see her wonderfully awful car in the driveway. Could Eric have sent him to the wrong house as a way to undercut him? No, people for the most part aren't that cruel.

The logical place to leave the long stretch of receipt paper was between the screen door and front door. That way when Katie did return home, she'd be sure to see it. Jeff folded it up very carefully, stepped out of his car and slowly crept his way to the front of the house. He was paranoid about her parents seeing him, wondering what some teenage boy was doing snooping around their home. As quietly as he could, Jeff opened the screen door, then even more quietly began to close it, lodging the paper in between. It left the door ever so slightly ajar, making it impossible for Katie to miss.

But what if she did miss it?

Don't think that way. There was nothing to do now but wait. And stress. And stress some more. Jeff had to get his mind off things. A distraction. Luckily, he knew of a party in Nissequogue that would be raging.

Jackie

"What happened, honey? Are you alright?"

Marie was mothering her. Jackie understood why. She was not alright.

Adam navigated the car down the winding dirt roads. Marie was looking back at Jackie, who was determined not to make eye contact. The car took many twists and turns through Nissequogue. Finally Marie took her eyes off Jackie and directed them forward, to see what was going on.

"Do you know where you're going?" Marie asked.

"Sure," Adam replied. "I'm taking a shortcut."

The car drove parallel to the river, then took a sharp left down a nameless road. This was followed by an even sharper right down a dark hill. Each bump caused the three of them to bounce high from their seats.

"I think we're in someone's driveway," Marie said.

"I know where I'm going. Relax," snapped Adam.

Where the hell were they? These desolate backroads were creepy enough during the day, but now at night they seemed terrifying. It felt like they were driving into the abyss.

POP!

"What the fuck was that?" Marie screamed.

The car started to slow down, making a thumping noise as it did.

"I think we blew a tire," Adam said.

He pulled the car over as far to the right as he could. Just along the edge of the tree line. Then he turned off the engine. Jackie had little reaction to this. It seemed like the logical next disaster of the night.

"Why are you stopping?" Marie asked.

"Because we blew a tire," he said again.

"We're in the middle of nowhere. Can't you at least drive us out of here?" Marie looked out the window into the dark woods.

"No. I'll fuck up my rims."

"Do you have a spare?"

"I have a donut, but it's pitch black out there."

"So?"

"I don't have a flashlight."

"So?"

"I won't be able to see. I need light to change a tire."

Adam turned off the engine. The car got quiet. All three passengers peered outside. They couldn't see anything. There was probably nothing to see, and if there was, who'd even want to see it? Scared, Marie locked her door.

"Is this safe?" Marie asked.

"Is what safe?" Adam asked.

"Being out here in the woods. I mean what if something happens to us?"

"What could happen?"

"Murderers. Bears."

"There's no bears on Long Island."

"There's bears at the Long Island Game Farm."

"That's a zoo."

"But there *are* wild animals in the woods."

"Squirrels and raccoons. Maybe deer. Maybe. Nothing that will hurt you."

"Opossums?"

"Probably."

"I'm scared of opossums."

What the fuck were these two talking about? Jackie couldn't listen to this conversation for much longer. Nor could she handle the way Marie put so much emphasis on the 'o' in opossum. If only someone would come rescue her. If only she had her father's useless car phone.

Suddenly there was silence. Not a sound from inside or outside the car. Not even an opossum. Jackie didn't expect it to last long. Marie was clearly trying to contemplate their situation. Adam must love this. Alone in the woods with a scared Marie Rossanda. Maybe tonight Adam would finally make that move he'd been building towards for the past five years. The only thing standing in his way was Jackie being there.

"So what's the plan?" Marie asked. You could tell she was nervous to hear the answer.

"I guess," Adam said, "we'll have to wait until the sun comes up so I can change the tire."

It wasn't even 2AM. Jackie was not going to wait until morning while these two talked about auto repair and wildlife. She flung open the back door and stepped out into the night.

Marie quickly rolled down her window and shouted at her. "Jackie! Where are you going?"

She didn't even turn around.

"You're going to get killed. Come back!"

Jackie kept walking into the blackness. Before long, the car, Marie and that inane banter were far behind.

What was she doing? Why had she done any of the things she'd done tonight?

It was so dark Jackie could barely see her hand in front of her face. She assumed if she kept walking this path she'd either hit a main road or the river. Either way she'd be able to follow it back to civilization...eventually.

T.J.

The Psych Center was in the rearview mirror. As they drove down the road, Liz didn't say a word. In fact, it'd been a good fifteen minutes since she'd last spoken. The silence forced T.J. to have cigarette after cigarette, filling the car with smoke.

"There's one more Yodel," T.J. said. "Who should we throw it at?"

"Whoever you want," Liz listlessly replied.

What had changed? I mean, T.J. knew what had changed but he couldn't figure out why she was suddenly acting this way.

"Are you alright?"

Liz just let out a sigh. T.J. needed to fix this. But how could he if he didn't know what was wrong?

"Did anyone ever tell you, you look like a cute dinosaur?" T.J. said this with the biggest possible smile on his face. Liz didn't even acknowledge him. She just stared out the window.

"Can you pull over?" she asked, gesturing towards the parking lot of a King Kullen supermarket. T.J. pulled in. Her wish, after all, was his command.

It was late, nearly one in the morning. Sage's party would still be going on. They could buy more Yodels and attack it. Yes, that might recapture the magic.

T.J. circled the near-empty parking lot before pulling into a spot right next to a beat-up white Toyota Camry. He knew the car. It belonged to the Hodrinsky twins, two skateboarders with shaved heads who spent their evenings in various parking lots drinking and doing hardflips or fliptricks or whatever. T.J. could never tell the difference between the skateboarding moves any more than he could tell the difference between the twins. You knew where they liked to skate because the lot would be filled with "Skateboarding Is Not A Crime" stickers.

The Hodrinskys seemed to be taking a break, just sitting on the curb in front of King Kullen, resting their feet on their boards, eating saltine crackers out of the box. Next to them was Jane. She was one of their girlfriends, but again, T.J. could never remember which one. She was holding a plastic bag with a goldfish in it.

"Wait here," Liz commanded. She marched past the twins, heading through the automatic doors of the twenty-four-hour market.

"Who's that?" Hodrinsky One asked.

"Liz...." Oh my God, did T.J. not know her last name? "Liz, she goes to Commack. She's friends with Seth. What's with the fish?"

"There's a carnival in Islip," Jane said. "I won it! It was one of those games where you have to throw a ping pong ball into a little fishbowl."

"He's not gonna make it," Hodrinsky Two chimed in. "How long can you live in one of those bags?"

"And where are we gonna keep it? Do we need a tank or something?" Hodrinsky One added.

"It could live in a cup of water or a pot," Jane argued.

"That's no way to fucking live," said Hodrinsky One. "We should put it out of its misery."

"Yeah. Just swimming back and forth in a glass, it's gonna be dead in a week. Less than a week," said Hodrinsky Two.

"Fine," relented Jane, "but how do we do it? Flush him? Then maybe he has a fighting chance in the sewer."

"I say burn him," suggested Hodrinsky Two. "A Viking funeral!"

While these three were debating the most humane way to murder a goldfish, T.J. was watching Liz through the window, at the counter. What was she buying? He was told to wait here but was starting to get worried about her. Fuck it, he went inside.

Liz seemed in a panic as she talked to another in a series of frustrated clerks.

"*You* must piss somewhere. Can't I just piss wherever that is?"

"The bathroom is closed to customers overnight," the clerk replied. "We've had too much vandalism."

"Vandalism?" Liz yelled. "It's pretty obvious why I need to use it. This is a fucking emergency!"

As T.J. approached the counter he saw what the "emergency" was. Liz was buying a home pregnancy test.

"What's up?" he asked.

Liz turned to him, fire in her eyes. "Jesus, I asked you to wait outside."

"Why are you buying a pregnancy test?" T.J. asked, concerned.

The clerk decided to step away, kindly leaving these two alone for their awkward moment.

"Because, I might be pregnant."

"I don't think it works that way."

"What are you talking about? We fucked. Duh."

"No," T.J. tried to explain. "I mean you can't be pregnant. We only had sex an hour ago. I think it's too early for a test to tell."

"Just…just let me put my mind at ease. Ok?"

"We used a condom—"

"That's not a hundred percent." Liz then turned towards the clerk who was just close enough to keep an eye on the situation. "I guess I'm just gonna have to pee on this in the gutter!"

Liz pushed past T.J. and out of King Kullen, pregnancy test in hand. T.J. was beyond confused. He knew that even if she was pregnant this test wouldn't show it. He also knew there was no way she was actually pregnant. It all felt so irrational.

By time T.J. caught up to Liz, she was standing at a payphone, punching in the long code from a calling card. Her eyes were welling up with tears. In the background he could hear the fish debate raging on.

"Maybe we should eat it. Goldfish filet," Hodrinsky One said. "That way it's part of the whole circle of life."

Liz began pleading into the phone. "Hey…it's me. I'm at the King Kullen in Smithtown…Can you come get me?"

She didn't have a crew anymore. Who was she calling? T.J. was starting to get frustrated. This magical night was falling apart.

Liz hung up the phone and turned to him. She was shaking.

"Someone is picking me up," she said. "You can go."

T.J was stunned. An hour ago he was falling in love.

"What did I do?" T.J. asked, desperation in his voice.

"You didn't *do* anything. I just need to go home."

"Let me drive you," he pleaded.

"What the fuck is wrong with you? I need you to leave! Please leave!" Liz was shouting now. Her face turned red as tears poured down it. "GO! FUCKING GO!"

Jane and the Hodrinskys were now watching. Embarrassment joined T.J.'s other emotions. Confusion. Frustration. Heartache. In his head he was already planning their second date and now she was screaming at him. He started to open his mouth to protest but she cut him off.

"Don't say anything. You keep trying to say shit to make it better. You talk too much."

Talk too much? T.J. was the quiet type. Matt Pace talks too much. Not T.J. Weber. Liz didn't understand who he was. T.J. looked like he wanted to punch something. Like he wanted to go into King Kullen and smash every item on the shelves. Rage built up inside him. T.J became as red as Liz.

"AHHHHHH!"

T.J. let out a monster scream into the night air. Then he slammed his fist into the side of his head. Again and again and again. Screaming the whole time. Jane and the Hodrinsky twins seemed taken aback, rising to their feet. Liz was completely unfazed. T.J gave himself one last strong whack in the front his skull. He was breathing heavily now. He wanted to hurt someone.

Marching towards Jane, T.J. ripped the goldfish bag out of her hands. With all his strength he hurled it straight up into the air. Time stood still as everyone watched. As the bag hit its peak point in the sky, it paused for a second. Did the goldfish understand what was about to happen? Of course not, it was just a stupid goldfish.

The bag came crashing down towards the earth with far more speed than it had risen. As it hit the pavement it exploded, splashing water everywhere. The twins and Jane ran to the spot it had landed. The goldfish lay there, still alive, gasping for air. Blood trickled past its gills.

"Woah," Jane said.

"T.J." Liz said, "You've got some real fucking issues. You should get help."

Without looking back, T.J. jumped into Seth's car and peeled out of the parking lot.

Jeff

It was always a pain in the butt driving through Nissequogue but this was far worse than usual. Not only were the darkened streets packed on either side, making it impossible to find parking near Sage's house, so many dirtbag teenagers were wandering down the center of the street you could barely pass through. Once Jeff did finally park, he started the long walk up to Sage's place. The home was lit up like Christmas. In fact they were the only lights you could see in the neighborhood. Music blasted at a level that carried deep into the night. Approaching the house, Jeff strolled past a sweet young girl urinating on the side of the road. There's no way the well-to-do denizens of Nissequogue would allow this behavior to go on much longer.

Crossing into Sage's back yard was like passing into a hedonistic version of a John Hughes film. Drunks vomiting into bushes, only to come back up for more booze. Boys and girls groping at one another, out in the open rather than in the shed like civilized folks. And teenage rebellious destruction. They were tagging the house and tearing apart lawn furniture. Someone had taken Sage's barbeque and thrown it into the swimming pool. Although it was far too cold for people to go in the pool, many sat around it, some on the diving board, dangling their feet over the edge. A surreal haze hung over as Björk's "Human Behavior" played, setting the proper mood.

Jeff wandered around, looking for an ally. He seemed to have so few tonight, and yet he knew everyone.

Usually.

For whatever reason this party was made up of unfamiliar faces. No T.J. No Jackie. Not even a Matt. Making Jeff feel even more out of place, he was still dressed in his white Movieland polo. He had extra clothes in the car but kept forgetting to change into them. He didn't look as foolish as he felt, but feeling foolish is always much worse.

Stepping inside things weren't any better. The white kitchen floor had become blackened. The cabinets had been ransacked of whatever they once contained. And Jell-O was *everywhere*. On the walls, on the ceiling, on people. Jeff was glad he'd missed whatever this was.

"Sage!"

Jeff finally spotted the party's host. She ran over, throwing her arms around him. "How crazy is this shit?" she said with glee in her voice.

"Who are all these people?" he asked.

"Beats me. I'm just so glad you made it!"

She began dancing around him. Not a care in the world. Worrying about how your home is destroyed and how your parents will murder you is a worry for tomorrow.

"Jackie was asking about you," Sage said.

"Is she here?"

"I just saw her leave. She looked upset. I think she's having problems with her new boyfriend." Sage twirled around, her dress spinning up ever so slightly.

"Damn, I would have really—"

Before Jeff could finish his thought, the party was over. Walking through Sage's front door were two of Suffolk County's finest. Tall. Strong. Intimidating.

"Cops!" someone yelled. Guests ran, fleeing like the rats they were, from a sinking party.

"Whose house is this?" one of the officers loudly asked. Sage twirled over towards the burly policeman.

"Mine. What's the problem?"

The cop was taken aback by the question.

"Well, for starters you're causing a disturbance in the community."

"We can lower the music," she innocently suggested.

"Your guests are trashing the whole neighborhood. They need to go. Now. Also there appears to be many intoxicated minors," the cop stated in his most authoritarian tone.

"They showed up that way," Sage politely rebutted.

"I need you to turn the music off. Then I need everyone who you want here to get inside and stay inside. Everyone not in your home in the next five minutes needs to go or we will place them under arrest."

This was Jeff's cue to leave. Sage would let him stay here all night if he wanted, but he wasn't in the mood for this. Maybe he'd head to the diner and get something to eat. A Belgian waffle or a cup of matzo ball soup.

He walked past the officers and into the front yard. Chaos. Kids running everywhere: Racing down the streets like madmen, jumping fences into other people's yards. All to get away from the cops. How many cops had come to break up this party? All of them. It was more police than Jeff had ever seen in his life. Now the light shining from Sage's party was partnered with the lights from dozens of police cars. Officers were grabbing teens, rounding them up and in some cases throwing them into a police wagon. These were Suffolk County cops. The highest-paid cops in the country with the least amount of actual work to do. They'd been waiting to bust up a party like this their whole lives.

Jeff slowly but deliberately headed down the road towards his car. He didn't want to draw any attention to himself. He had no reason to fear the cops, he hadn't done anything wrong, and yet he feared the cops.

Stepping into his car, he started the engine and slowly pulled out into the road. It was even harder to navigate than before. Police chasing down teens, racing in front of Jeff's vehicle. Logically, and legally, the dirtbags running away were in the wrong. They'd trashed a house, caused a scene and disrupted order. Still, Jeff rooted for them to get away. Screw the cops. We're young. This happens. It's teen spirit.

Suddenly Jeff slammed on the brakes. It wasn't a kid or a cop that blocked his path. It was garbage. Someone had knocked over all the garbage cans from the side of the road into the center of the road. It being too narrow to drive around, Jeff was stuck.

With an annoyed sigh, Jeff stepped out of his car. He walked to the cans and began dragging them back over to the side of the road. Then from the bushes he heard a voice.

"Yo. Yo, man."

Jeff turned to see three guys step out of the bushes and into the street. They wore baggy clothes, low-hanging pants and sideways baseball caps. Three more middle-class white suburban kids who pretended to be black. It was fine if you wanted to emulate or admire black culture, but it always rubbed Jeff the wrong way that these people had no real desire to try and understand it. Jeff knew enough to know that he didn't relate to the black experience and never would. He hoped acknowledging that fact was considered being respectful. He'd been able to watch the L.A. riots three thousand miles away on his television with empathy, avoiding judgment. What did these three guys really think of the culture they were appropriating? Had they even seen *Do the Right Thing*?

"Yo, man. There are cops everywhere. You gots to drive us outta here."

"What?" Jeff replied, confused.

"Five-O is everywhere. Please, man." The one doing the asking was clearly the leader. The guy to his left looked sheepish, standing unsure of himself, a poser who probably questioned if he really belonged with this crew. The guy to his right, however, looked insane. Big bulging bug eyes. A fixed, psychotic smile. Was he high or just crazy? Probably both. He carried a backpack. What was inside? God only knows.

"No," Jeff said matter-of-factly.

The leader looked at the car, then at Jeff, sizing him up.

"Thanks, man."

And with that the three of them made a beeline to the car. They opened the door, the leader and poser piling into the back seat while Bug Eyes took shotgun. Jeff stood there, mouth agape. Could they just do that? Could they just get into someone else's car like this?

Jeff marched over. It'd been a lousy evening and he needed it to end.

"Get out of my car!"

"Please," the leader begged. "There cops everywhere. Just drive us to the end of the road."

Jeff didn't know what else he could do. The end of the road. That wasn't so bad. What could go wrong?

"The end of the road?" Jeff asked.

"Just the end of the road," the leader answered.

The three of them nodded enthusiastically as Jeff sat in the driver's seat. Who knows, maybe these guys aren't so bad. Yes, they were forcing Jeff into this situation, but that doesn't mean they'd hurt him.

Jeff started the car down the narrow dirt road. Then Bug Eyes began shaking back and forth in his seat with excitement.

"I knew you'd do us a favor because I'd do you a favor. We do each other favors, that's what we do!"

Jeff decided to ignore this burst of enthusiasm and concentrate on the road. He had been looking for something to get his mind off things, and this certainly was accomplishing that. Driving, they passed more and more police cars. How many cops did Smithtown even have? After a few minutes they reached the intersection at the end of the road. Jeff came to a complete stop.

"Get out!" Jeff demanded.

"Man," the fearless leader whined. "You said you'd drive us to the yacht club!"

"The yacht club?!?"

"Yeah. That's where our car's at."

The yacht club was miles away down a series of dark, twisting roads. Jeff was not going to the yacht club.

"Why did you park at the yacht club?"

Before Jeff could get an answer, a police officer tapped on his window. The boys got real still as Jeff rolled it down. He needed these people out of his car and saw an opportunity.

"You can't stop here," the officer said. "You're holding up traffic."

Jeff peeked in his rearview mirror. There was currently no one behind him. He decided to plead his case.

"Officer—"

"Move it. Now!"

"Officer, let me explain. These guys just forced their way into my—"

"I don't care. Move your car or you're gettin' a ticket!"

So much for the police being helpful. Everything Jeff had learned in the D.A.R.E. program had been a lie. There was no choice but to keep driving with these hoodlums in the car. Turn left towards the yacht club, towards certain danger, or right towards the diner, towards certain deliciousness. Jeff turned right.

"I'm going to the diner and so are you," Jeff informed them.

"Please man," the leader again implored. "Just take us to River Road. We'll walk to the yacht club down River Road."

"River Road?" Jeff questioned.

River Road wasn't that far out of the way. It met up with the main roads, so Jeff could drop them off in a safer, well-lit, high-traffic area. He headed towards the new destination.

The crazy one in the passenger's seat began rolling down the window, letting in the cool night air. Then he reached into his backpack and began pulling out bottles of beer. Don't crack open a beer. All Jeff needed was to be pulled over with an open container in the car. Not to worry. Instead Bug Eyes decided to dispose of his underage alcoholic evidence.

A bottle flew from the car, hitting the pavement with a crash. Then he threw another bottle. And another. CRASH! CRASH! The sound of bottles breaking was all Jeff heard as he sped down the street.

Finally the intersection of River Road was in sight. The anger was building within Jeff. Earlier this rage was reserved only for Nick, but now he channeled it towards his uninvited guests. Pulling into the middle of the intersection, blocking traffic in all four directions, Jeff slammed on the brakes.

"GET OUT!"

"Man," the leader started as calm as can be. "You said you'd drive us to the end of River Road."

"THE END OF RIVER ROAD?!?"

Cars began honking. Jeff had to make a decision. Just get them there. They'll get out then. Get them there and be rid of them. So he turned down River Road.

River Road is the darkest winding road in all of Nissequogue. Maybe on all of Long Island. Jeff was now on it, angry, chauffeuring his three would-be murderers. Rage filled his eyes. Everything today had gone wrong. Everything that might be or not be, depended on how this ride ended. Sensing the change in mood, the two boys in the back got quiet. Bug Eyes, however, either too drunk or too stupid to realize this, began talking. He started giving Jeff the third degree.

"Yo man, you got a job?"

Jeff didn't answer. Obviously he had a job. He was wearing a Movieland polo shirt. Did this guy think this was how he dressed normally? Stupid.

"Yo, you go to school?"

Jeff didn't answer. Obviously he went to school. They had been at a high school party. How old did this guy think he was? Stupid.

"Yo, you got a girl?"

The Nick betrayal had been hours ago and Jeff hadn't talked to anyone about it. It was a complicated and confusing situation. He wanted to let it all out. Explain to someone how hurt and frustrated he was. Jeff wanted a truly unbiased opinion from someone totally outside the situation. Why not Bug Eyes? Maybe it was kismet that these three got in his car. Yes. Tell him everything. Spill your guts.

"Well, there's this girl and she just got out of a relationship and—"

"I gets it, man," Bug Eyes interrupted. "You know why? Cause I've been sucked off more times than you've ever pissed. I've been sucked off and I suck off and I'm gonna suck you off!"

What. The. Hell. Did this nutjob just say that? Oh my God, Jeff was about to be raped.

"It's not that kind of ride, buddy." Jeff said this firmly to let Bug Eyes know no one was going to suck anyone off tonight. But he also tried to frame it in a comical way to let Bug Eyes off the hook in case it was only a joke and not oddly aggressive, latent homosexuality. Jeff looked in the mirror to see what the poser and leader were doing. They were wide-eyed, equally confused by what was happening.

Jeff reached the end of River Road. Desolate. He spun the car around, bringing it to a halt.

"GEEEEET OUUUUUT!"

The boys in the back said "thanks" and swiftly climbed out. But Bug Eyes lingered, staring at Jeff, who was trying hard to keep his eyes forward. Jeff was angrier than he had ever been. He was breathing heavily. Red-faced. He took a breath and repeated himself as calmly as he could.

"Get out."

Bug Eyes stepped out but didn't close the door. Instead he leaned back inside, extending his hand for a high-five. Not out of the woods yet, and not wanting to piss off a crazy person, Jeff responded with a half-assed high-five.

"Thanks man," Bug Eyes said, his words sounding more and more slurred. He didn't remove his hand. Instead he kept high-fiving Jeff, over and over again. "Let me…let me touch your face."

Not waiting for a response, Bug Eyes began to caress the side of Jeff's face. Jeff squirmed in his seat, unsure of what to do. Here in the woods by a river, it was just like *Deliverance* on WPIX.

"Let me touch your face…let me choke you!"

On a dime, Bug Eyes turned violent. He gripped his hand around Jeff's throat and began to squeeze.

At that moment Jeff saw his life flash before his eyes. He would never get to be with Katie. Never grow old. Have kids. This was it.

But Jeff was in a car. And Bug Eyes wasn't.

Jeff stepped on the gas. Bug Eyes was knocked backwards, off his feet and out of the vehicle. The door slammed shut. Jeff sped down the road, away from his would-be rapist. In the rearview he saw Bug Eyes jump up and down like Yosemite Sam, shaking his fist in the air. Ever so faintly Jeff could hear screams of "I'll kill you! I'll fucking kill you!"

Just like that Jeff was back on track, headed towards the diner for that Belgian waffle.

T.J.

If it hadn't been so late, T.J. surely would have killed someone. He was speeding down suburban side streets like a madman, swerving all over the road. Where was he going? Where could he go? He couldn't show up at a party like this. If only Jeff had a beeper, he could contact him and find out where he was. Jeff had a way of putting things like this in perspective. Taking a chance, T.J. sped past Jeff's house. His car was missing. He's probably at the party. Wait, hadn't Jeff mentioned something about the girl from Hot Topic? He probably hooked up with her. Of course he did. Everything would always work out perfect for Jeff fucking Rosenduft.

T.J. got back onto a main road. Nesconset Highway. The cigarette hanging from his lips was down to the filter. He flicked the butt out the window. If he kept speeding he'd get pulled over by the cops. Good. The perfect end to a perfect night.

In his rage, T.J. hadn't even noticed the radio was off. Now he became painfully aware of an eerie silence which only emphasized how alone he really was. Music would calm him down. He turned the knob of the stereo. The next track on Liz's Tom Waits album clicked on.

This was not what T.J. wanted to hear. The lyrics felt longing, regretful, pained. It was about her. About how her wildness had made him feel free. About how her laugh had made his heart soar. About what it had felt like to be inside her.

T.J. burst into tears. This was stupid. He was romanticizing her all out of proportion. He'd been so lonely and could only envision a future full of loneliness.

Up the road he saw a figure, slowly walking. Its head hanging low. Why would anyone be wandering the side of a highway in the middle of the night? T.J. saw this as an opportunity to snap out of his malaise. He leaned across the seat and rolled down the passenger-side window. Then he grabbed the last Yodel.

Slowing down, T.J. took aim at his final victim....

Jackie

There was a girl Jackie knew in passing. This girl liked to put pictures and phrases on buttons and t-shirts. Jackie had seen her selling this merch at a show. She was pretty sure the girl also worked at Hot Topic.

One night after a Freaks performance Jackie asked if she could make her a special shirt. She offered to pay but the girl did the job for free. It was a tight white t-shirt, with bold red lettering that said "Jackie Spam Has AIDS." Jackie thought this shirt was the sickest thing. She loved it, looked at it almost every morning. No one knew she owned this shirt. One day she planned to march into school wearing it. She imagined the shocked looks she'd get. But every morning, rather than put it on, she always carefully placed it back at the bottom of her dresser drawer.

Maybe Monday morning she'd finally wear it.

Jackie must have been walking for thirty minutes. She was cold. Tired. However, there was no choice but to press on.

All of a sudden the road lit up. Startled, Jackie turned around. A pair of headlights approached her. She peered towards them, squinting, nearly blinded. Oh, fuck. Marie was right. Jackie should never have left the car. She was about to be murdered.

Logically Jackie knew she wasn't going to be murdered. There hadn't been a murder in Smithtown since some kid was killed behind Dogwood Elementary before she was even born. And Jackie wasn't totally sure if that story was true. It would be a fitting end to her high school legacy; to be killed shortly after giving Nick LeWinter a handjob in a shed at a party. Yes, she was probably about to be murdered.

The lights got closer and closer. Jackie stood her ground. Bracing herself for whatever came next.

Matt

Matt was wrong. He knew it. But were his crimes so bad as to be subjected to this? Stranded on the side of the road, miles away from home. Even if he found a payphone, who would he call? Jeff? His mom? Matt would never consider hitchhiking, mostly because of a story he once heard about some kid who was murdered behind an elementary school. There was no other option, he'd have to walk all the way home. It would only take a few hours. What time was it? Just keep moving.

How long had he been walking? Had it even been an hour? Suddenly he heard a car fast approaching. This car wasn't like the others on the highway. Its engine revved faster. Its lights shined directly on him. Was this car gunning for him?

Matt turned around and, startled, jumped back. The car was starting to slow down but was still practically on top of him. What to do? Run? Where would he go? He swallowed hard as the car rolled up beside him.

"T.J.?"

T.J. Weber glared at Matt. He was holding what looked like a Yodel. Matt couldn't be sure, it was far too dark to tell.

"What the fuck are you doing out here?" T.J. asked.

"I was abandoned. Left for dead. Can you give me a ride home? Please."

Matt could see the wheels turning in T.J.'s head. Then he put down the Yodel and motioned for Matt to get in.

"Thank you." Matt was so happy that he clearly forgot this was the man who sent his evening down such a dark path in the first place. And wait a second, was T.J. about to nail him with more baked goods?

Matt buckled up as T.J. continued down the road, heading into town. The stereo played a slow song with gravelly vocals. Then Matt noticed something that took him aback. T.J.'s eyes were red. His cheeks looked wet.

"Were you crying?" Matt asked.

Immediately T.J. turned to Matt, pain in his face. "Fuck you!" he said.

Matt could have pushed the issue. If not for T.J., he'd have lost his virginity. But there was also something so human about this moment. Matt had never seen T.J. vulnerable before. Had anyone? He decided to let it go.

"So," T.J. started, "what happened? Shouldn't you be with that girl? Did she ditch you?" T.J. giggled a little at this thought, and Matt suddenly seemed foolish for feeling sorry for him.

"No," Matt answered. "If you must know…you know what, this is all your fault."

"My fault? What's my fault?" T.J. asked, incredulous.

"You threw those Crappy Doodles at me and my whole day went to shit."

"What happed to the girl?"

"Well, I was really upset. And embarrassed. We were watching *Reservoir Dogs*. And she gets on top of me, starts kissing me. But I was so upset about what happened I just didn't want to anymore.

So I pushed her off of me and said, 'I just want to watch the movie.' And she stormed out!"

Matt confessed this to T.J. of all people. T.J. would tell everyone and the world would know Matt turned down sex to watch *Reservoir Dogs* for the one-millionth time. The car was silent. And then, T.J. let out the biggest laugh Matt had ever heard.

"It's not funny," Matt said.

"It's fucking hilarious! You pushed her off you? Why would you do that?"

"I was upset!"

"You were *that* upset? Bullshit."

"Don't tell anyone," Matt pleaded.

"Oh, I'm telling *everyone*. Why would you even tell me that? Why would you tell anyone that? Lie at least."

"I don't know, T.J. I honestly don't know why I pushed her off. I was scared. But you and your fucking Crappy Doodle cupcakes didn't help."

Now Matt was the one on the verge of tears.

They pulled up to a red light. Matt felt T.J.'s eyes on him. The mood of the car had changed. No one was laughing. Matt turned to T.J. There seemed to be actual sympathy coming from him.

"Things didn't work out with my girl tonight either," T.J. admitted.

"What happened?" Matt asked.

"After we dropped you off we started throwing Yodels at people.... Hey! Do you wanna throw the last Yodel?"

"Throw the Yodel?"

"Yeah. It's only fair."

T.J. handed Matt the last Yodel.

"What do I do?" Matt asked.

"Throw it at whatever you like."

"Just throw it?"

"Yeah. Oh," T.J. almost forgot the most important part, "and when you throw it you have to yell yodelayheehoo."

An hour ago, hell, maybe five minutes ago, Matt would have thought about hurling it right in T.J.'s face. But for the first time in all the years they'd hung out, it felt like a real friendship. He didn't want to blow it. Instead he began peering out the window, looking for a target.

A shiny Mercedes turned onto their street, heading in the opposite direction. They were stopped at a light and the Mercedes had come to a crawl in order to take the sharp turn. It was a perfect shot, like the Kennedy assassination. Matt leaned out the window.

"Yodelayheehoo!"

The last Yodel flew high into the air. A perfect arc that sailed over their car, heading directly for the Mercedes. Maybe Matt had better hand-eye coordination than he gave himself credit for?

SPLAT!

The Yodel smashed dead center on the windshield. An explosion of cream filling.

"Nice!" T.J. shouted.

Matt exuded a bizarre sense of pride. Through this low-level act of vandalism he was accepted for the first time in a long time.

The Mercedes slammed on the brakes, coming to a stop right next to Seth Feldman's shitty Honda. They couldn't see through the Mercedes' tinted windows, but they didn't have to. They knew whoever was inside was pissed.

"Fuck," T.J. said.

The light turned green and T.J. hit the gas, speeding down the road. Matt turned around to see what the Mercedes was doing. Holy shit! The Mercedes spun around fast and started following them.

"They're following us!" Matt said in a panic.

The old Honda was no match for whatever was under that Mercedes' hood. Before too long it was riding their tail. Honking its horn. Flashing its brights.

"What the fuck is wrong with this guy?" T.J. asked.

The crazed Mercedes was close enough to bump them. It wouldn't, would it? If the driver had wanted just a license plate number, he'd already gotten close enough to get it. He wanted to hurt them.

They had to get off the main road. T.J. turned into a residential neighborhood. He sped as fast as he could through the winding streets. Matt grabbed the 'oh shit handle' and quietly started to pray. Dying in a fiery auto crash after throwing a Yodel? Yup, this seemed like the way he was destined to go. He'd never make things right with Rebecca. He'd never make things right with Tariq.

T.J. was making some evasive maneuvers. He was even attempting fake-outs, motioning the car to make a left, only to quickly turn right. No matter what they did, they couldn't shake the Mercedes. They were actually in a high-speed chase! Maybe Steven Spielberg's best film was *Duel*.

After racing through neighborhoods for a good five minutes, they found themselves on top of Dogwood Drive, one of Smithtown's steepest hills. They were eye level with the town's water tower. The Mercedes still on their heels, there was no place to go but down.

The Honda began to shake as it picked up downhill speed. Matt felt sick in the pit of his stomach, like on a rollercoaster. He couldn't see the speedometer, but there was no way this piece of shit car should be going this fast.

They were nearing the bottom of the hill, but T.J. was struggling to keep the wheel steady as it vibrated wildly. The Mercedes was right on top of them. And then, T.J. lost the wheel. About thirty feet from the bottom, he just couldn't hold it steady any longer. They veered off the road and off the hill. Not down the hill. *Off*. The car was airborne.

Time stopped. Everything felt light. Everything was in slow motion. Matt held his breath. There was no time to do anything else. There was no time to react. This was it.

And then...

BOOM!

The car came crashing down at the bottom of the hill. All four tires blew out at once from the pressure of landing on them hard. The Honda skidded perfectly to the side of the road, scraping its rims against the pavement. It came to a stop. A perfect parking job.

Matt and T.J. looked at each other. They were alive.

Then, remembering the chase, they quickly looked up at the hill. Thirty feet above them, where they had flown off, were the headlights of the Mercedes. Still. In the quiet of the night they could hear the killer car's engine running. Should they run? Escape into the neighborhood on foot? Then the Mercedes began to slowly back up, turn around and drive off. Its work here was done.

*****

Matt sat on the side of the road, still in shock about what had happened. Many cars drove by but none stopped because the Honda didn't look like it had been in an accident. It looked like it was simply parked on the side of the road. On closer inspection someone might notice all four tires were flat. On even closer inspection they'd see the rims were trashed. On *even closer* inspection they'd see the axles were bent to fuck. This car was totaled.

"FUCK!" T.J. screamed. "What the fuck am I gonna tell Seth?"

"He's got insurance, right?" Matt asked.

"What good will that do? He wasn't driving."

"The cops won't know that. I say we leave it here, walk to a payphone, tell Seth what happened and *he* reports it. He'll tell them he was driving."

"Won't his insurance go up?" T.J. questioned.

"Maybe. But far less than if an uninsured driver was driving," Matt reasoned.

"I guess that makes sense. But what the fuck do we know? Neither of us owns a fucking car."

T.J. was right. Matt didn't know what he was talking about. It sounded right though. And really, what other option was there? Matt decided to stay calm for the both of them.

"Either way," Matt continued, "we need to get to a phone. The Millennium is about a twenty-minute walk. Let's go there, call Seth and get something to eat."

T.J. thought about it, finally giving Matt a nod of approval. He reached into the car and pulled out his cigarettes. He popped one in his mouth, lighting it.

The pair began the walk towards the Millennium, neither saying a word. Then Matt looked back over his shoulder. He saw the hill they'd been racing down and then the spot they landed. A weird grin formed across his face. A sudden burst of pride and excitement.

"T.J., we were airborne."

T.J. smiled back. He looked almost giddy. "Fuck yeah we were!"

Jeff

Jeff had felt alone before but now he was really alone. Driving to a diner by himself on a Friday night. No one to share his misery with. No one to eat his feelings away with. And where the hell was he? He'd lived in Smithtown all his life but still found these wooded backroads confusing. He didn't want to drive himself in a circle and come across Bug Eyes again. There were murderers wandering these woods.

Then, out of nowhere, a figure walking ahead on the side of the road. Jeff drove towards it. The figure stopped and turned towards the car, balling its fists, preparing for a fight. Is that a girl? It's not safe for a girl to be out here at night. Is that...

"Jackie?" he said to himself.

Jeff slowly pulled up beside her and rolled down his window. Cautiously, Jackie peered inside. Relief poured over her face.

"Jeff! Thank God!"

"What are you doing out here? Did you run from the cops?" Jeff asked.

"What?"

"Were you at Sage's party?"

"Yeah. It's been a weird night," she said.

The two looked at each other. Their eyes tired. Their faces long.

"Do you want to get in or do you want to keep walking through the woods alone at 2AM?"

Jackie smiled. She opened the door and jumped inside.

"So," Jeff asked, "what happened?"

"I'm not in the mood," she said. "Can we just go to the diner or something?"

Jackie didn't want to talk about whatever had happened. Jeff obviously wanted to ask, particularly about where her college boyfriend was. But he couldn't push, or worse, come off as gloating, so instead he decided to finally open up about the Katie situation. As they drove to the diner Jackie listened, reacting most viscerally to the parts about Nick. As they pulled into the parking lot, he finished his tale.

"I stepped on the gas and he went flying out of the car, screaming. And then I found you."

"Holy shit!" Jackie exclaimed. "You've got to put that in one of your movies."

Jeff was so busy trying to survive it hadn't occurred to him how the experience could translate to art.

Jeff parked the car. They sat in the Millennium Diner parking lot, quietly smiling at each other. Neither seemed ready to go inside.

"Jeff, can I ask you something?"

"Of course," he said.

"Why did you want to date me so bad?"

Jeff was surprised by the question. It seemed a total non sequitur and he wasn't really prepared to answer.

"I'm not sure how to answer that. I mean, why wouldn't I have wanted to date you? You're beautiful and smart. You're my best friend. I guess the most important thing was that you're confident. You know who you are and don't give a damn."

Jackie looked down, shaking her head.

"I give a damn. I do."

The mood in the car shifted. Jackie was clearly uncomfortable with Jeff's answer. He'd meant it as a compliment. Even if Jackie cared deeply about what her idiotic classmates thought of her, the fact she didn't let them know it still made her someone to admire. A goddamn hero.

"Can I ask you something then?" he asked. "Why *didn't* you want to date me?"

"I just didn't, alright. I don't know why. You're great. You're *my* best friend."

"Then why can't I find a girlfriend?" he questioned.

"I honestly don't know. You're funny, cute. Hey, maybe it will work out with Katie. Stranger things have happened?"

They laughed, looking into each other's eyes. Smiling.

"Jeff, can I ask you another question? It's really important."

"Of course." Jeff said this in his most serious tone of voice. Was Jackie about to open up about the events of her evening?

"Do you believe in dinosaurs?"

This was even more of a non sequitur. Jeff began to laugh at the bizarreness of the question. Jackie wasn't laughing. She was dead serious. Her stern look caused Jeff to awkwardly tense up.

"Who doesn't believe in dinosaurs?" Jeff said.

They continued to stare at each other. A long, poignant pause. The moment felt intimate. What is happening? Should he kiss her? Is that what this is about or is it a total misreading of the situation? In that second Jeff had an opportunity. The girl he once spent eighteen blissful days with seemed to be letting him back in, if only for a moment. Had their terrible evenings finally pushed them back together? Jeff started to inch towards her, so slightly he might not have been moving at all. Jackie didn't move towards him but didn't move away either. Move in and kiss her. She's all you ever really wanted.

No. Not anymore. The small torch Jeff carried had finally been extinguished. Katie was all he ever really wanted now. Would he get her? Unclear. But he wasn't going to ruin his chances by doing something both he and Jackie would regret.

Jeff broke off eye contact and turned his gaze towards the diner. Jackie did the same. It's possible the moment hadn't happened at all. Either way, it had passed.

Squinting through his windshield Jeff saw something in the diner window he'd never in a millennium expected to see.

"Is that T.J...with Matt Pace?"

Millennium

Long Island is a diner culture. Every town on Long Island has at least one, if not two. For Jeff, Jackie, Matt and T.J. these diners were where their evenings would always end. The diners of Long Island were where they could have their long rambling talks about culture and love. Where they could chain smoke and drink coffee until dawn. Diners were the place where everyone knew their names. If you had nowhere else to go, you could count on someone you knew being at the diner to welcome you into their booth.

Diner-hopping was a favorite activity for the group. They'd hit up three or four in a night. Share some appetizers at the Candlelight, a main course at the Hauppauge Place and dessert all the way out at the California on Sunrise Highway. Or sometimes it was just a new cup of coffee, and only coffee, at each place they went. You could get away with that at the diners on Long Island, as long as you didn't mind a dirty look from the owner as he rang up a six-dollar check for four people.

Hopping from diner to diner, the crew would notice similarities that gave them all a warm familiar feeling. No matter how unique the layout or the staff or the way they prepared the food, some things never changed. The same endless novel of a menu. The same cheap paper placemats advertising local doctors, attorneys and mechanics. The same jukeboxes at every booth playing the same selection of Billy Joel songs. The same terrible coleslaw that no one would ever touch and yet it still came free with every meal. The same autographed photo of Telly Savalas behind the cash register, signed predictably "Who Loves Ya Baby," reminding you that Greeks had a monopoly on the diner business. They were all open twenty-four hours a day, three hundred sixty-five days a year.

In fact many of the owners claimed the keys to the place didn't exist. Is there anything as reliable as a Long Island diner?

Millennium. That was Smithtown's diner and thus the crew's spot. If they said "let's go to the diner" it only meant Millennium. After a movie, Rock N Bowl or a night at lesser restaurants, they would always come home. Although it was a surprise to find Matt and T.J. sharing a booth, it was not a surprise that this foursome would all find their way here at the end of an eventful evening.

"…and a mosquito is just a shitty, hated creature. Teenagers are shitty, hated creatures. And libido? I mean, it's pretty fucking obvious we can't control ourselves."

Jeff began to nod in agreement with Matt's analysis. Even Jackie and T.J. had been open to hearing it, as they smoked their last cigarettes. For three-thirty in the morning, the smoking section was surprisingly empty.

The waitress brought over their food. A Belgian waffle for Jeff. A piece of lemon meringue pie for Jackie. A side of fries for Matt. And for T.J., his order as of late, a veggie burger with bacon. Three months ago, the Millennium added veggie burgers to their menu to keep up with the ever-evolving dietary culture. T.J. had been disturbed by this development. He believed burgers were something made of meat and vegetarians were "pussies." So he'd ruin a veggie burger by adding bacon, thus spitting in the face of vegetarians. The added bonus was the confused look he'd often get from waitresses when ordering.

"Can we all now agree?" Jackie asked. "Kurt *was* the voice of our generation. Not Trent Reznor or Eddie Vedder. It was Kurt and Kurt alone."

"I don't agree," T.J. said. Jackie threw her hands up in frustration. This time T.J. was talking sincerely. "No, Jackie, I'm not trying to be an asshole. I'm just saying I'm part of this generation too and he doesn't speak to me."

"You're literally 'Smells Like Teen Spirit.' You're everything Matt just said that song is about," Jackie argued.

"Why do I need a fucking label?" T.J. fired back.

"I don't think you have a choice," Matt chimed in. "You don't get to pick what defines your generation. My parents weren't hippies but they still grew up surrounded by hippie music. It's what made their era unique. Twenty-five years later people see them as the Woodstock generation and there's nothing they can do. Twenty-five years from now your kids will see you as the Nirvana generation."

"Fuck that!" T.J protested. "For all you know Kurt won't stand the test of time."

"Yes he will," Jackie said defiantly.

"Why?" T.J. asked.

"Because he died," Jeff said, finally joining in the discussion. "And because he was great. You know he was, T.J. Just because you didn't like his music doesn't mean it wasn't great music that inspired almost everyone who heard it. Gangsta rap isn't my thing but I can acknowledge Ice Cube is really talented."

T.J. struggled to come up with a counterargument. From the strained look on his face it was clear he was trying *really* hard.

"I'm proud to have someone as smart and sensitive as Kurt Cobain represent our generation," Jackie added.

"Wait," T.J. interjected. "Ice Cube? N.W.A.? Don't they speak for a generation of black people in a way Nirvana never could?" He had finally found his argument and he was obviously proud of it.

"Are you saying black people can't relate to Nirvana?" Jackie was raising her voice.

"I'm just saying they relate to Niggas Wit Attitudes a lot more."

Now it was Jackie left searching for a counterpoint.

"Maybe no generation is defined by one type of music," Jeff offered, trying to make peace. "My parents love The Beatles and Dylan equally. Can't they both be the voice of a generation?"

"Our voice is Kurt, though," Jackie said.

"Angsty, white suburban teens? Yeah, we're Kurt," Jeff agreed.

"Billy Joel," blurted Matt. Everyone stared, confused. Undaunted, Matt continued his point. "We all like Billy Joel, or at least did at one time. We've all been to Billy Joel concerts. Why can't he be our voice?"

"Our voice needs to be a contemporary," Jeff tried to remind him.

"We're from Long Island," Matt argued. "We grew up on him. I'm just saying you all know every word to 'Only the Good Die Young' but I doubt you know all the words to 'Heart-Shaped Box.'"

"I know all the words to 'Heart-Shaped Box,'" Jackie shot back.

"So do I," Jeff added.

Matt slunk down in the booth, embarrassed he brought up his favorite musician.

"I know all the words to 'Only the Good Die Young,'" T.J. offered. "It's a good fucking song. It's about sex and angst too."

Suddenly Matt shot back up. T.J. had come to his defense, and it almost made up for the Crappy Doodles.

It'd been over a year since this particular group of people had a conversation like this. One of those debates that send you deep into the night. A debate with no real winner or answer. They kept arguing, not to reach any conclusion, but because it was the most fun they'd had together in a long time. There wouldn't be too many more of these. Maybe there wouldn't be any more at all.

"I got it!" Jeff shouted. "I fucking got it!"

Jeff's cursing took the whole table by shock. It was the first time they ever heard him say "fuck." Whatever he came up with, it had to be good.

"Ba-da-bop-ba-da-bap...bom."

There were no words, just a tune everyone immediately knew. A tune that brought a smile to the faces of everyone in Jeff's generation. It wasn't full of angst. It was full of joy, nostalgia and even wonder. It was the theme to *Super Mario Bros.*

Jackie, Matt and T.J. joined in, "singing" along. Ten years ago, like most children, they'd all been given Nintendo as a present. It was everyone's favorite gift, an 8-bit arcade right in their living room. And every Nintendo came with a copy of *Super Mario Bros.* The first thing they all heard when they powered up their system for its maiden playing experience was this theme. Every child of the 80's related to that moment. Even if they couldn't afford a system or their parents wouldn't let them have one, they could still think of this music and dream.

Over the years video games got more advanced and the graphics better. Nintendo was just the beginning. Not for gaming but for technology in general. These four had seen cassettes become CDs. Telephones put in cars. A device you could wear so anyone could contact you at any time. A machine that printed out photos of Winona Ryder. Their generation was becoming consumed by technology and it was beginning to define them.

But not today.

And not tonight.

For right now, despite the death of an icon, nothing had changed.

Nirvana

They had spent hours at the Millennium talking, laughing and reminiscing. The sun was finally starting to come up, and sadly it was time to go. Where had all the time gone? Where had high school gone?

The crew piled into Jeff's car and one by one he drove them home. On the ride, for whatever reason, all conversation stopped. Instead they sat in silence, listening to whatever track came next on whatever mixtape was playing. They weren't tired. They weren't sick of each other. They just didn't know how to express what they were feeling. This was the end. The surreal, dreamlike lyrics of Beck echoed through the car and their minds. He sang of morgues, toilets that overflowed and dildos that crushed the sun.

*****

T.J was the first to get dropped off. He bounded out of the car and headed straight for his garage. He typed in the code to open the door. As it violently cranked upward he started to worry he might wake his mom. Without a key, this was the only way inside.

He headed upstairs, into his room, throwing himself down onto the bed. His bed was just a box spring and mattress. The floor was more a hamper, covered with an array of dirty clothes. As the morning sun started to creep inside, layers of dust were made visible. Posters of cult metal bands and horror films covered the walls.

Liz. T.J had shared something special with her, even if it was only for one night. He reached down, picking a dirty sock up from the floor. T.J. loved her beautiful dinosaur face. He could still smell her on his clothes. It had felt good to be inside her.

251

*****

Jackie thanked Jeff for the ride and the rescue from a woods full of opossums. When she walked through the door she was surprised to see her mother already awake, sitting at the kitchen table, drinking tea and eating an English muffin. Usually Jackie's mom would give her a hard time for coming home so late, or early as it were. Instead she just told Jackie "goodnight," with a smile. In the morning Jackie would need to ask her mother for a ride to get her car. Would she tell her why?

When she got to her room, Jackie opened up the bottom drawer of her dresser. Underneath her sweaters was the t-shirt she had commissioned from Katie. Jackie pulled it out, laid it on the bed and stared at it for a long time. A smile crept across her face. Who gives a damn? Monday morning she would wear it to school. Monday morning Jackie Spam would have AIDS.

*****

Matt was last. As he walked through his front door he noticed something on the frame. With his finger he wiped at it. Cream filling. He couldn't help but laugh.

Maybe it was the four cups of coffee he had at the diner, but Matt was wired. He went downstairs and continued to watch *Reservoir Dogs*. Matt smiled as the cop was getting his ear cut off. This film was too good to be ruined by any dumb girl. Tomorrow he'd have to find a way to salvage what was left of his friendship with Tariq.

*****

As he pulled up, Jeff couldn't believe what he saw. A beat-up Oldsmobile with ridiculous painted-on flames parked in front of his house. He pulled over and jumped out so fast, he forgot to turn off the engine. Calm down. Don't be so eager.

Katie walked towards him and they met in the middle of the street.

"I just came by to tell you that Eric Hodrinsky won the essay contest," she said with a smile.

"Oh, did he?" Jeff replied.

"Yeah. It was just some real next-level writing."

"Maybe he should try getting it published."

"I've already sent it to *The New Yorker*."

Jeff wanted to grab her and kiss her but he was enjoying the playful banter too much.

"How did you know where I live?" Jeff asked.

"The phonebook," Katie said matter-of-factly.

The phonebook! Why didn't Jeff think of that?

"I hope you weren't waiting long," he said.

"A few hours. It gave me time to make you something."

From her pocket Katie pulled out a small box. The kind of department store box you'd put earrings or a necklace in. She handed it to him. Jeff started to open it, but Katie stopped him.

"Don't open it until I'm gone," Katie requested. "Wait until I'm out of sight. O.k.?"

"O.k."

Jeff stood there holding the box. He desperately wanted to know what was inside. He wanted to know more than he'd ever wanted to know anything in his life.

Katie strolled back to her car, then before getting inside, she turned to Jeff.

"What if you met the girl of your dreams, she's perfect in every way except she can't shave her legs."

"Why can't she shave her legs?" Jeff asked.

"It's a medical condition, her skin is too sensitive and if she tries to shave them she'll just bleed all over the place. So she has really hairy legs. Like thick Sasquatch hair. But the rest of her is perfect. Can you still date her?"

Jeff didn't have to think about it.

"If I love her, I think I can learn to live with hairy legs."

"That's gross." Katie laughed, then got into her gaudy Oldsmobile and pulled away.

The mixtape in Jeff's car started a new track. "Lithium." As the opening notes began, Jeff realized this was the first Nirvana song he had heard all day. How was that possible?

Katie's car was at least two blocks away, but Jeff still wouldn't open the box. If he opened it now, she'd never know. And he wanted to open it so badly. But he loved her and he had promised to wait until she was out of sight. When you love someone you keep your promises to them. Even the stupid ones.

Katie's car became smaller and smaller until it finally disappeared.

Immediately Jeff pulled the top off of the box. Another button. Simple and yet it was Katie's best work to date. Plain white with black lettering.

Will you go out with me?

Jeff smiled. The chorus to "Lithium" kicked in.

Acknowledgments

When taking on any creative endeavor it is impossible to do so without support from friends and family. For me, that obviously begins with my mom and dad, who have always supported me through everything.

An extra special thank you to Lorenzo Manetti and Melody Rock, who not only read multiple drafts of this novel but willingly listened to me ramble and stress about it deep into many nights.

For advice, assistance and various hookups, a thank you to Alex Stein, Rachel Karten, Megan Hayes, Rebecca Miller, Ant Fallon, Bob Blankenheim and Carrick Bartle.

Finally, thank you to the best podcast partner anyone could have, Sean David, and the best writing partner anyone could have, Jarrod Garcia. Working with both of you over the years has always kept the creative juices flowing.

About the Author

Will Link was born and raised on Long Island before moving to Los Angeles in 2005. He has been a filmmaker, screenwriter, essayist, critic, podcaster and performer. *Crazy About Kurt* is his first novel. Feel free to contact him via Twitter @TheRealWillLink

Made in the USA
Middletown, DE
12 July 2019